RETURN TO
Autumn

JOHN RICHARDS

ISBN-13: 978-0692793411
ISBN-10: 0692793410
johnrichardsauthor.com
JR Press

CONTENTS

CHAPTER ONE

The Beginning of Summer

EVERY YEAR ON THE LAST day of school it was our ritual to exit the school bus by jumping out of the emergency exit in the back. Mark, Joey, and I had been doing it since we were in sixth grade. Irritating the bus driver went back further than the sixth grade though. In third grade when we had a substitute bus driver that didn't know the route, we would yell, "That's it! That's my house!" This shouldn't have mattered since the driver was only supposed to stop and let us out at designated stops. Nonetheless, she slammed on the brakes and jerked the bus to a halt and we hid behind the tall-backed green seats calling out "Why are you stopping?" or "NO! Not here you idiot." The woman just sat there looking back at all us kids in her huge rearview mirror, stunned and trying to figure out if someone was actually going to get off. Someone would eventually tell her no one was getting off, and she would start driving again to the chorus of our profanity. The bus was so full she wouldn't have a clue who was doing all the yelling, and in hindsight, I don't think she cared who was yelling. She just wanted off the bus herself. Now, we were juniors in high school. Even though we all had our driver's licenses we couldn't drive to school until we were seniors due to limited parking spaces.

You could only jump out the back of the bus on the last day of school. If you did the jump midyear, the principal would be waiting on the bus after school the next day and the bus wouldn't leave for home until he found out who had activated the fire exit. He would threaten to give everyone a detention if nobody tattled or confessed. I know because we tried to do it on a Friday once in eighth grade, and the next Monday there he was waiting for us inside the bus. Carolyn Autumn was the one who told on us. She didn't even hesitate; she wanted to get home and 'prepare' for a history test she had the next week. Carolyn was constantly worrying and studying. She lived down the street from us and we rode the bus together since our first grade year.

"I'm sorry Adam," she said. "I had to. I thought I was going to fail."

But she was one of the most successful students in school. She was always on the honor roll, as long as I could remember anyway. Her obsessive worrying was likely the reason for all her success in school.

When we performed the fire exit jump we usually did it at a stop where we knew about ten kids needed to get off. Mostly just to add to the confusion. The bus would come to a stop and the three of us would be in the very back, ready to make our escape. This time as the bus jerked to a stop, Joey lifted the emergency handle and the shrill door alarm went off. BRRRRRRING. Out we jumped and off we sprinted. In years past we would have someone close the door behind us and halt the alarm, but through experience we found it was much more fun to have the bus driver walk back to shut the door. And so in our usual fashion the summer of 1992 began; the three of us running from an angry faced bus driver glaring out the back door. The bus driver's response varied each year, but this year to our delight, it was to give us the finger.

We always walked home from the bus stop together. Mark and I lived about ten houses away from each other and Joey lived in the neighborhood behind ours. After our successful jump, we resumed our standard walk-home banter.

"Dude, you should have seen it last night," Mark said.

"Did you see Christine last night?" I asked, knowing exactly where this was going.

"Oh dude, it was crazy," he said.

"OHHH MAN," Joey said in his goofy voice, all excited like a little kid. "What happened? You have got to tell me what happened."

"It was like bam bam," Mark said, pretending to swat at something in front of him at about waist level.

"What did you guys do?" I asked, knowing full well the story I would get would be outrageous and mostly untrue.

"Did you give it to her?" Joey asked excitedly.

Mark began, "Okay dude, here's what happened. I went over to Christine's house last night after my pump." Mark was always referring to the way he looked after he lifted weights as his pump. "Her mom was gone and we had the house to ourselves."

"Oh man!" Joey said.

"I started kissing her in the kitchen and getting her hot, I mean really hot. She got so worked up she grabbed my shirt and started pulling me to her bedroom. So here I am sitting on her bed, and BAM! Her tits are like gewww," Mark said pretending to fondle Christine's breasts. "You should have seen them in this shirt she had on."

"Oh man, you rock!" Joey said.

"Go on," I prodded, preparing for the bullshit ahead.

"So I get her on the bed," Mark said. "She pulls off my shirt and she climbs on top of me. I had just done like seventy-five push-ups in her bathroom on the sly so my pump was like bam!" he said as he made the muscles in his upper body flex tightly. "She yanks her shirt off and I reach back behind her with one hand and unfasten her bra and work her tits at the same time. Dude, it was smooth as hell!"

"Were the lights on?" Joey asked.

"Nah, but you could still see everything," Mark said. "Her boobs are like gewww! You should have seen'em. So anyway, at this point she is so into it that she starts grinding on me and I mean hard. We were grinding for like three hours. She must have had like five or six orgasms."

"How can you tell?" Joey asked.

"Oh man, you just know. Plus, she was practically screaming, dude."

"Did you get off?" I asked Mark, looking over at Joey who was getting way too excited by this conversation.

"Oh yeah, I came like three times," he said "My underwear was full!"

"Good Lord," I said under my breath, envisioning what this would entail. Somehow picturing Mark with a full load in his pants made me think this may have actually happened.

"And the worst part is, when I went to take a piss today at school, I thought I had herpes."

"WHAT?" I asked "Why the hell would you think that?"

"Dude, I have this big ass scab on my ween," he said more quietly.

"What the fuck?" I asked, turning to him and squinting my eyes.

"It was the grinding dude, she rubbed it raw," he explained.

"OH MAN!" Joey exclaimed.

Now it's not that I doubted Mark and Christine had grinded the way he said they had, but parts of his stories were always exaggerated. I doubted she was the one that initiated the pull into her bedroom. I also didn't see her pulling his shirt off, and the orgasms? Mark probably did mess his underwear several times, but I'm not so sure about Christine. If she was moaning or carrying on, it was because Mark was riding her like a bull I imagined. Mark had too many stories about girls that I had never met. He would have had some great pump and the girl would always be ravishing him and pulling off some article of his clothing. He would be doing her as he held her up against the wall. There were always several orgasms too.

I saw relationships with girls very differently than Mark. He was just plain savage; unable to control his urges like a wild animal; a wild pig with nothing but dropping a load on his mind. I was looking for a companion. Sex was up there on my list, but part of the allure was being with someone I respected. Admittedly, Mark had more experience with girls than I had at the beginning of the summer of 1992, but that would quickly change.

CHAPTER TWO

French Kissing and Second Base

THE MOST I HAD DONE up to that point was French kiss and feel a girl up. The French kiss came months before the feeling up, but both during my sophomore year. Neither went very smoothly. I had spent countless hours thinking about doing both since the seventh grade, as every boy does. I was dating Becky Hasting for a whole month before we French kissed. I was nervous as Becky was considered by some as an old pro at it. She was not my first French kiss, but by rights she should have been.

I was friends with a girl named Cynthia who I hung out with most days after school. Her mom worked so we usually had the place to ourselves. One afternoon she and I decided it would be a good idea if we practiced our French kissing. The reason we needed this practice was because I had just started dating Becky and she had just started dating a boy named Zack, and it had been awhile for both of us since we last kissed anyone. I never let on to her that I had actually never kissed a girl before, and she acted as if she had had plenty of kissing experience, so it was no big deal. To be honest, I think this was a first for both of us. It was also the only time I had ever cheated on a girl.

"Soooo, should we practice?" she asked as we were sitting on the couch in her living room.

"Sure," I replied nonchalantly.

"K. I'll be right back," she said as she hopped up off the couch and ran into the other room. Moments later she sprung back into the room and flopped onto the couch next to me, lying back with her head on a pillow. I looked down at her and she smiled back up at me. Too many moments passed I assume because she grabbed the bill of my baseball cap and pulled my face down to hers. Our tongues met and I finally understood what was so special about French kissing. Girls are soft, and taste sweet like cherries! I tasted her mouth and tongue in amazement. Fantastic, I thought. I wondered what I tasted like. Probably not like cherry.

I didn't attempt to engage Cynthia in 'feeling up' practice. That happened with Becky Hasting when we were at her house with a few of Becky's friends. Her best friend Sarah took me aside in private and asked with a big smile,

"Have you gone to second base with Becky yet?" knowing full well we hadn't.

"Nah, not yet. I don't think she's ready," I replied.

"That's not what she says."

Instantly my heart started pumping harder and I felt the blood rush from my head. "Why, what did she say?" I asked.

"She wants you to, you know, feel her up."

"That's cool," I said, trying to act like it was nothing. "Did she say how she wanted to do it?" As I had no idea how to do it myself, I thought I would ask. I had always heard from other guys that they did it with the lights off.

"No, she didn't say. So are you going to do it today with her?" she asked with a big smile lighting up her face.

"Yeah, probably," I said. "We'll see how things go."

After about an hour of uncomfortable conversation between the girls in the living room and me sitting quietly on the couch, *she* asked me if I wanted to go into the other room with her. Her bedroom. Her mom wasn't home; she never was. She was a flight attendant and worked odd hours. What could I say to her? No? I would look like a pussy. Plus what excuse would I have not to? I was nervous, but agreed. She led me by the hand into her bedroom and we awkwardly lay down on her bed. I still hadn't mastered the art of French kissing with Becky. In fact, I didn't enjoy it at all, and in hindsight I doubted there could ever be any mastering the art of French kissing with Becky Hasting.

Another great realization and disappointment in life regarding the female sex came from kissing Becky. I realized that all girls did NOT taste sweet and like cherries. The only reason Cynthia tasted like cherries I later realized was because her favorite candy was Twizzlers and she was constantly eating them. The way I would know Becky wanted to kiss was by her coming at me from a few feet away with her mouth already propped open. It was as sudden as that. Of course, at times I would expect it and knew it was coming, like when my Dad drove her home at night after spending the day at our house. I walked her to the door where we stepped inside and closed the door. I dreaded dropping her off. The attack was always sudden and intense. I imagined her as a lizard or snake the way her tongue flicked in and out of her mouth and into mine. I had learned about the Jacobson organ in school. It is located on the roof of the mouth in certain reptiles and used in conjunction with the tongue as a sensing tool. Snakes use their Jacobson organ to find their prey. Was I prey to Becky Hasting? It certainly felt like it sometimes. I tried to avoid the kissing whenever possible with Becky, but dreamed about it with other girls.

So there we were, lying on her bed in intense silence. I couldn't wait to feel her tits but was terrified, and highly agitated at the thought of having to endure what could end up being an hour of French kissing. However, as I had been waiting for this moment for so long, I knew I had to feel her up. The room was bright as could be with the lights glaring down from above the bed.

"What about the lights?" I asked.

"What do you mean?"

"Well, don't you want it to be dark?"

"I don't care," she said. Now I was really confused. I had always heard you did this in the dark and here we were in her bright bedroom lying on our sides staring at each other. I reached out and put my hand up the back of her shirt and started fumbling around with her bra strap. She smiled at me after a few long and awkward seconds.

"Here, let me help you." She sat up and put her hands up the front of her shirt and undid the clasp. I didn't even know that there were bras with snaps in the front.

"Thanks," I said with a smile as she lay back down flat on her back. And there we lay. Me on my side with my hand up her shirt playing with her breasts, and her lying on her back staring up at the ceiling. Her breasts were actually quite large for her age, an early developer. Looking back I realize how utterly ridiculous this must have felt for her. I didn't kiss her. I couldn't bring myself to suffer that level of punishment during what would be my first experience feeling a girl's breasts. Not having a clue what I was doing, I needed to concentrate. I felt her up in silence for about twenty minutes, but I can't remember how the whole ordeal wrapped up. Sure it was uncomfortable as hell, but I enjoyed it just the same. It was my first time. I finally had something to tell Mark about. Hell, I might even have embellished the story a bit.

CHAPTER THREE

Home

WHEN I OPENED THE DOOR to my house the delicious scent of freshly baked apple pie wafted out the door and filled my nose. My father was always baking something. Apple pie was his specialty, but he would also make cheesecakes, strudels, cookies and fresh breads. They were good too. He definitely had a knack for baking.

"Smells good, Dad," I yelled as I kicked my shoes off onto the rug and walked into the kitchen. It was one of my dad's rules. You had to take your shoes off at the door. My father kept a clean house.

"Adam, I made apple pie," he said as if the smell could be mistaken.

"Where's John?" I asked.

"Sleeping, of course." It was probably a good thing too. John, my older brother who was home from Purdue for the summer, was one of the most ornery sons-of-bitches I had ever had the privilege of knowing. I know he loved me and he truly believed the beatings he gave me were for my own good, that they were in some way helping me become more of a man.

"You know your brother is in your corner," my father would always say if I ever dared to complain about him.

"Why don't you go down and see your brother?" my dad asked right off the bat.

"Dad, I don't feel like it. He just got home. I'll have plenty of time to see him," I pleaded.

"Do you want to hurt his feelings, Adam?" he asked. "How would he feel if you didn't even bother to go say hello after he's been gone for so long?"

"Fine," I said as I slumped over to the basement door next to the kitchen. I crept down the stairs cautiously, trying to not wake John if he was still asleep. I slowly inched the door open and peered into his room at his neon beer signs on the wall and his imported beer bottle collection lining the window wells. I walked in to find my brother sitting at his computer desk playing a computer game. The room stank of sweaty gym shoes and socks.

"John?" I said softly.

"Don't you knock, you fucker?" he said, twirling around in his chair and getting up from his desk, an evil gleam lighting his eyes. I took a step back towards the stairs. "Come here and give your brother a hug!" This command had me backing up more quickly as he started to charge straight for me. I spun on my heels and leapt up the stairs three at a time. After the second or third stride, I glanced back over my shoulder only to see him bracing himself with his hands on both railings and propelling himself and his foot up behind me, aiming straight for my groin. I tried to clench my buttocks but since I was taking such long strides I was left completely exposed. It all happened in a split second.

"Karate chop!" I heard him holler as his foot caught me dead on the balls and wiener. A perfectly placed shot, he would later reminisce. As I lay there cradling my aching balls, I wondered why I hadn't just trusted my instincts and stayed clear of him. That night, as the pain in my testicles pulsed to the beat of my heart I wondered if I was ever going to be able to have children. A shot like that, I thought, could cause some serious permanent damage.

There was no point in telling on John when he gave me my 'daily beatings' as he called them. If my father did believe me, it would just make the beatings come with greater frequency and intensity. Looking back on the beatings, I suppose they were character building. I've learned to take a good shot and get right back up again.

Not only did my dad, William Raynor, bake desserts; he cooked breakfast, lunch and dinner too. He made the beds each morning, did the laundry, dusted, vacuumed, did the dishes and crocheted. He was a "housewife," Mark would say, but to us he was just Dad - a stay at home dad. He was good at it too. Many people have the impression that a stay at home dad is a lazy dad. Not ours, he kept an immaculate house. When we came home from school there would be a freshly baked pie on the counter, or freshly cut cheese, sausage and crackers on the table with a vase of flowers lit up by a nice votive candle. The crocheting was kind of hard to get used to. I would come in with Mark and Joey in tow, and my dad would be sitting in the living room off the kitchen crocheting. Mark would say "Hey Mr. R! What you up to?" as if he didn't know. My dad had no shame. He would simply explain he was working on a blanket for his nephew, or a scarf for John or me. Joey would just stand there with his usual goofy look. "Ahh," Mark would say, as if it was normal for a man his age to be crocheting while watching baseball. To mom, John, and myself it was normal.

Mary Ferguson-Raynor, my mother, was a respected businesswoman in our town. St. Charles, Illinois, is located about an hour and twenty minutes outside of Chicago if traffic was cooperating. A suburb thought to be charming by the majority. Mom was an attorney with an established law practice when she met my father. This is the reason for the hyphenated last name. "Everyone already knew me as Mary Ferguson," my mother said whenever we asked why she had two last names when we were young. My father always told us, "Your mother's one of a kind, boys, that's why. A real keeper." We were a normal family, if there is such a thing. We went to church every Sunday growing up; John and I were both confirmed Catholics. We were raised to be 'young educated gentlemen,' in my father's words. We were too. Any variance from the path my parents headed us down was no fault of theirs.

My mother could have been home more while I was growing up. In fact, my mother wasn't around very much at all, and if she was, she was working at her desk. She had her own office in the house. She left for the firm before we were up in the morning. She did her best to be home for dinners though. Who could blame her when dad was such a great cook? He didn't just make a few good dishes and put them into rotation. He made something new several nights a week. He found new recipes in the paper, or from his subscriptions to *Bon Appétit* or *Readers Digest*. "Your mother works her arse off," he would say. "The least I can do is have a good meal waiting for her when she gets home." Mark mentioned that my parents had their roles reversed. However, if he had tasted my mother's cooking, which thankfully I had rarely ever done, he wouldn't think so.

Friday night my father had cooked a wonderful

dinner; breaded artichokes to start, chicken cordon bleu, wild rice, and for dessert, the apple pie.

"It's nice to have you home, John," mother said as we sat down at the table. All of us except Dad of course; he was always the last one to sit down. He served us. My mother sometimes pretended she was going to help and would say, "Oh you sit, Will. Let me get it," and halfway stand up. But Dad always refused and she sat back down. I don't think she ever really meant it when she offered to get whatever it was Dad was serving, but she still offered and did her half stand up thing at the table.

"Adam's having pains in his groin, Dad," John said right off. Dad was the kind of person who took unexplained aches and pains very seriously. He always wanted to take us to the doctor right away, or even the emergency room. His cousin Rudy had a brain aneurism and Dad said that, a few days before he died, he'd complained of a headache. Dr. Jakes, our family doctor, must have loved Dad because we kept the man in business. I hated going to see Dr. Jakes. Most kids don't enjoy going to the doctor, but most kids also didn't live in constant fear of having to potentially visit one on a weekly basis. Stuffed up nose? Call Dr. Jakes. Fall down and bump your head? "We need to have Dr. Jakes take a look at this one. It's the shape of the bump that is concerning me." Cousin Rudy's sudden aneurism really did a number on my father. If it weren't for that damn aneurism poor Dr. Jakes would have likely starved.

"I'm okay," I told Dad to reassure him. I knew he'd be calling Dr. Jakes first thing if I didn't end this now. Dr. Jakes would say, "Interesting. I better have a look right away." It was true though, I was having pains in my groin. What Dad didn't know was the pain was from the beating my brother had given me. If I told my father about kick to my groin I would likely get another one or something worse. I wouldn't just forget what he did though. I would plot my revenge, never doubt that. "So do you have a summer job yet?" I asked John, knowing that he didn't and that my parents wanted him to work over the summer.

"I'm filling out applications now," he said confidently. "How about you?" he countered. "When I was your age I was working."

"That's right, Adam, you're old enough now," Mom said. "You should go to the Grocery tomorrow and get an application."

"Mom, I am NOT working at the Grocery. It's for dorks," I said.

"John worked there when he was your age," she said.

"I know. That's my point, Mom. I can't work there," I said, looking at John who was now grinning at what he had begun. "They hire retarded people to do the bagging.

That happens to also be the very job they give you when you first start working there. Do you want everyone in the town to think I'm retarded?"

"Don't be so insensitive Adam," Mom said as John did his best facial impression of a mentally disabled person. I did feel bad for being insensitive, but also wasn't as confident as I would like to be.

"You know what happened to cousin Rudy, don't you?" my father asked, changing the topic back to my aching groin.

"Dad, I'm okay," I repeated with a sigh.

"I think you should call Dr. Jakes," John said with a smirk in my direction.

"If you're not feeling better by tomorrow morning, I want you to tell me. This isn't something to mess around with. You've only got one shot," Dad said. Ironic how without John's shot to my balls I wouldn't have the pain in my groin in the first place.

"I know what I want to do for work this summer anyway," I added, bringing the subject of conversation back onto safer ground.

"And what's that?" Dad asked.

"I'm going to do yard work around the neighborhood," I replied. "I'm going to print up flyers and put them out this weekend. Mow lawns and stuff."

"Well, if you can make it pay it sounds fine to me," Mom said.

After dinner I went up to my room and worked on a flyer for my yard business. I would charge a flat rate of ten dollars an hour. I was actually excited about this now. At about nine in the evening I had a whole bunch of flyers printed out. I wanted to get them out right away; so I took off on my bike and put them on the side of the mailboxes in my neighborhood. I had about a third of them leftover by the time I got back home, but it was a start and I was exhausted.

I was woken on the first day of my first full week of summer vacation by the smell of sizzling bacon and a sweet, cinnamon something. I opened my eyes and glanced at my poster of Arnold Schwarzenegger all pumped up, hanging on the back of my bedroom door. I'd been lifting weights for the last six months and I was starting to get some good results. My body no longer looked like a little boy's, and I knew it. Whenever the opportunity arose I went shirtless. I wanted other people to see my results as well, especially the girls. I stood up, stretched, and walked over to my bathroom door. When I opened it the stink of putrid urine assailed my nose. Gross! If you forgot to flush the toilet in the summer the heat from the sun shining in through the window made the urine fester in the toilet, creating a hell of a stench.

Holding my nose, I sprinted over to the toilet, flushed it and sprinted back out again, closing the door behind me. I would just have to pee downstairs.

"You ready for some breakfast?" my dad asked as I entered the kitchen.

"Yeah, smells good," I said. I sat down at the table and started thumbing through the *Chicago Tribune*.

"I've got some good news," my dad said.

"What's that?" I asked as I took a sip of Dad's freshly squeezed orange juice.

"I spoke to Mrs. Autumn this morning and she got one of your flyers and has some yard work you could do."

I wasn't thrilled about working for the mother of the girl who told on us for jumping out the back of the bus all those years ago. The Autumn's had a massive backyard with a swimming pool and a guesthouse tucked away at the back of it. Mr. Autumn was not living there anymore due to the divorce. The yard had gone to shit, at least in relative terms to the other lawns in the neighborhood. The bushes were overgrown and the lawn was always too long. The backyard was over an acre and abutted a pond. Mark, Joey, and I had hopped in the Autumn's pool too many times to count over the years, always late at night when they were sleeping.

"Where did you see Mrs. Autumn?" I asked.

"In the produce aisle," he said.

I found it surprising that Mrs. Autumn would want me to do yard work for her. I was sure Carolyn had told her about our antics with the bus drivers throughout the years - although maybe she hadn't. Carolyn was a sweet girl but also rather quiet.

"When does she want me to come by?" I asked.

"She didn't specify, but I would guess soon. She said she would rather pay someone from the neighborhood to do it than someone she didn't know." My father set a plate of bacon, eggs and cinnamon toast down in front of me; the eggs were over easy, just how I liked them. I dipped my bacon in the yolk of one of the eggs, took a bite, and looked up just in time to see our neighbor, Mr. Berry, standing in our backyard with his dog. He was looking around, making sure no-one was watching while his dog was taking a crap on our lawn.

"Dad," I said. He looked over at me from the sink where he was washing up and I pointed to the backyard. My dad peered out the window and saw Mr. Berry with his golden retriever squatting in a four-point stance. A fierce scowl took over his features.

"Unacceptable," my dad hollered as he stormed towards the door. When Mr. Berry heard my father whipping the door open, he yanked on the leash and the dog went hopping along in his four-point stance finishing his business, leaving a three or four foot poop trail in his wake. I heard Mr. Berry guiltily promise my father that he would pick up the poop. I could hear my father explaining the issue with the poop residue. "It's not the poop that's the problem," Dad always said. "It's the residue left behind. What about bare feet?" No one in my family dared walk around the yard in bare feet. With neighbors like Mr. Berry and his dog Scooter, we knew better. My father came back in shaking his head in frustration. "That man's a nuisance, a complete giasticutis," he said. As Dad was not one for swearing, he made up his own words. "It sounds bad... it sounds like a swear word," he would say. I don't know when Mr. Berry was planning on picking up the poop that Scooter so kindly left behind in our yard, but it wasn't soon enough because my father was always the one picking it up. "I'll have to get it when it cools off," Dad said. He hated picking up a 'steaming turd', as he called it.

"So what exactly does Mrs. Autumn want done?" I asked.

"She wants a stump removed to start. I'm not sure what else. You'll have to iron out the details with her," he said. "You should stop by today and get things going."

I jogged back upstairs to my room after gulping down my breakfast, hoping the stink of fetid urine had dissipated. Thankfully it had, so I turned on the water in the shower and let it run while I stood in front of the mirror flexing my muscles, checking out my chest. My biceps were bigger than Mark's, but his pecks were bigger than mine. I was trying to catch up. Joey was skinnier than both of us. He hadn't hit his growth stage yet. He lifted and lifted but never gained any weight or sprouted any new muscle growth. Looking in the mirror, I took great pleasure in the progress. The workouts were definitely paying off. I took my shower, paying extra attention to my balls to make sure the kick that John had taken to them hadn't caused any permanent damage. On close inspection I decided I would be okay.

I found it fortunate that I could start my summer work doing odd jobs for Mrs. Autumn. Hell, I would get a wicked tan doing all the outdoor work too. Being my own boss for the summer would allow me to work as hard or as often as I liked, freeing up my spare time to hang out with my friends and goof around. My parents didn't want me to work only because of the money. My mom was a successful lawyer. We had plenty of money to go around. We lived in a neighborhood with large houses and big yards. My mom used to quote Hemingway, saying that this was a 'neighborhood of wide lawns and narrow minds'. They wanted me to understand the value of work, earn my own spending money and learn how to be responsible. I didn't mind. I wasn't afraid of a bit of hard work. Even though my parents were well off that didn't mean they gave us anything we wanted. In fact, John and I always had to work for what we wanted. We did odd jobs around the house to earn our spending money. Mow the lawn, wash the outside of the windows, weed the garden, wash and wax the cars, or in the winter shovel the walks and driveway. There wasn't a shortage of concrete to clear. Our drive was wide and long and there was plenty of sidewalk to shovel as well.

It somehow seemed as if it would be more rewarding doing work for other people. More like a real job, not just Mom and Dad's allowance money. If I worked twenty hours a week, that would be $800 a month. I would be taking cash in hand, tax free. Hell, I could buy a car with that much money a month. My parents let me borrow their cars when I needed to but wanted me to buy my own car. And I wanted to too. What young guy doesn't want his own ride? I would only do twenty hours though, and on my own terms.

Mark and Joey didn't have to work. Joey's parents didn't make as much money as ours did. He was the kid that would come over and raid your refrigerator if you let him. At his house, you would eat at designated meal times. No snacking in between, not to mention there was nothing to snack on at his house. My father did his best to make up for this. Every time Joey was over, my dad pushed food on him like the proverbial drug dealer, and

Joey was always up for eating. I was always up for getting out of the house as quickly as possible.

Mark spent most of his days at the pool, in the gym, or in front of the T.V. drinking Mountain Dew and eating au gratin potato chips. He exclusively ate au gratin potato chips. It was obsessive. Whenever I was over (which was often) there would be a bag of chips close by. Periodically he would grab a handful of chips and insert one whole chip in his mouth at a time. This was done repeatedly, always in the same fashion. I asked him about the chips and why he ate them so much, and he got offended as if I had violated sacred ground.

"It's just a snack, dude! Who doesn't eat potato chips? Besides, they're fucking good," he said. For the rest of that day he was quiet and reserved. When Joey and I were together without Mark we talked about the chips. We both thought it was odd and funny how obsessive he was about them. After the bus dropped us off after school Joey and I sometimes hung out, but Mark would have to go right home and take a break before he came back out. He was going home to have a snack, he would say. We knew what he was going to do. He was going to eat the chips. Mark walked home and Joey and I stood there where the bus dropped us off and made jokes about what Mark was doing at home with the chips.

"I bet he fills the bathtub with au gratins and jerks off in there," I said.

"No, dude!" Joey countered. "He's going to put his mom's bra on and stuff it with chips." This type of rant would continue on, sometimes for a half hour or so. It never got old. It was really amazing how many odd situations we could put Mark in with those chips. We only did this behind Mark's back mainly because it was such a sensitive issue for him, whereas we teased him about his mother's breasts to his face. Joey and I were in agreement that his mother had the largest breasts in the neighborhood. This earned us a stiff punch in the arm every time we brought it up. Mrs. Autumn, we all agreed, had the nicest set. The au gratins though, were off limits. We didn't want to hurt Mark's feelings.

We got our summer work out passes at the gym and pumped iron for a while, comparing and competing. Mark gave extra attention to his biceps, and I worked my pecks extra hard. Both of us were trying to even out our physiques - my smaller pecks and his smaller biceps. Joey just spent the time trying to get any kind of pump that he possibly could. By eleven in the morning Mark was satisfied he was fully pumped and ready to hit the pool, a mile walk from the community health club. The trick was to get to the pool while Mark still maintained his pump. Sometimes, we would have to wait to go into the pool until Mark knocked out another set of pushups to refresh his pump.

The pool was packed as we expected. It seemed as though more than half our high school class was there. Days like these were the greatest we had encountered in our short summers. Watching our friends play volleyball on the two sand courts and discussing the girls we were into. We played sometimes, but mostly we were just as happy to sit on the benches and chat. Christine (the girl who caused Mark's scabs or at least contributed to them) was playing volleyball. She was on the team at school and she was very good. She never spoke to us, and seemed to avoid Mark in particular. She was most likely still freaked out about their make out session. Mark must have been pretty intense, if what he said was true.

We all knew this might be one of the last summers like this. We had discussed it at length. College was coming up fast and we knew we would be separated. I always got better grades than Mark and Joey. Only because I didn't have to try very hard to get good grades. It came pretty easily to me. If I paid attention in class and studied for an hour or so prior to a test, I generally got an A or B. I wanted to go to a prestigious writing school; University of California or University of Iowa were among my top picks. I loved to read, and wanted to write. Since I was little I kept a journal. I had used one consistently since the third grade. I labeled them and kept them in a lockbox in my closet. I used them as diaries, and for my short stories and poetry. I had taken all the creative writing courses I could at school, which consisted of three semesters. Next year as a senior, I will have the opportunity to be a teacher's assistant for the creative writing classes. Joey was planning on joining the Navy as his father had. He planned on being away for a few years after high school. Mark was not considering college at this point. His dad was a general contractor and he would be able to start working for his father's business after graduation. We made a pact to stay best friends though.

Summer was the time of a boy's life when something exciting could happen. I had read Mark Twain. I had seen *Stand by Me*. I had romanticized those adventure stories. I wanted to share in those experiences, to have something spectacular happen to me. I've long since realized that when you least expect it, something amazing can happen. I remember in those books they would sit together by a fire smoking corncob pipes or stolen cigarettes without a care in the world. These experiences were what life was all about. Spectacular experiences, that's what I wanted. I came to realize that if you looked hard enough for what you wanted in life, you could find it. I would be starting my new summer job, doing yard work for Mrs. Autumn tomorrow. My searching would most certainly pay off.

Working Man

Loud Mexican music rattled me awake. The Mexican station always forced me out of bed. I went downstairs for breakfast, which Dad had already prepared. A plate of blueberry muffins and some freshly sliced cantaloupe this time. I listened to my father rant on for twenty minutes about Mr. Berry's dog, Scooter. After wolfing down my breakfast and hearing my dad out (you never walked out on him in the middle of a rant) I showered and put on some of my oldest clothes that I didn't mind getting dirty.

I walked over to Mrs. Autumn's, which was close by but out of sight from my house. The Autumns lived five houses past Mark's and as I walked past I imagined him still asleep, dead to the world. I wondered if Mrs. Autumn would supply the yard tools I needed to do the work or if I would have to bring the stuff myself. I reached her house, a white two-story colonial with a three-car attached garage on the side.

In my enthusiasm I bounded up to the open front door and rang the doorbell. After waiting patiently for a few seconds I peered in trying to see if anyone was home. I could see straight down the hall and out the back patio door where I spotted Carolyn Autumn lying on a lawn chair in the sun. I sniffed the inside of the house through the screen. It had no scent. A good sign. If there's no scent, the people are like you. If there is a scent, they're a bit off. I always found comfort in visiting somewhere if there was no unusual scent, especially if it was a sleep over. I could hear music faintly drifting through the screen doors. No one came to the door so I headed around the side of the house to the back yard where the pool was located.

As I rounded the back of the house I could make out that the song 'Hook' by Blues Traveler was playing on the radio. Carolyn was lying on her back in a white string bikini next to the pool, with a drink on the table next to her. To my utter surprise she wasn't studying and she was tan. I didn't expect it because I'd never seen her at the public pool before. But then, she did have one in her back yard so I guess she didn't have a need to go to the public pool very often. It looked like she was drinking iced tea and the glass had condensation dripping down the sides and looked deliciously refreshing.

It was hot out and I was already perspiring. I hated that. Mark and I always commiserated about how we would get done showering and the damn humidity would be so bad we'd instantly be sweating and we'd feel like we needed to shower again. In an upright chair a few feet from Carolyn, sitting at a long glass table with her back to me, was another girl talking on the phone. I approached feeling a little intrusive, especially since Carolyn was in her bikini.

"Carolyn," I said softly so as not to startle her. She sat up a little and put her hand over her eyes to shield them from the glare of the sun.

"Adam?"

"How's it going?" I said. The girl in the chair turned around, and I realized it wasn't a girl at all, it was Mrs. Autumn.

"Fine, what's going on?"

"Your mom said she needed work done," I told her, trying to look casual and hide that I felt stupid standing there. I also didn't want her to notice I was staring at her body. She was still squinting and shielding her eyes from the sun so she couldn't tell I was gawking at her.

"I've had enough work done, thank you," her mother said, laughing while on the phone. I gawked at her and felt my face heat up. I glanced back down at Carolyn as Mrs. Autumn became engrossed in conversation again. Carolyn just shook her head with a hint of a smile on her lips. When you thought of Carolyn Autumn, sexy wasn't the word that came to mind. Brainy, or reserved maybe, but not sexy, and here I was looking down at her and she was really fucking hot. Her dark hair hung straight and gently brushed her shoulders and chest. Her breasts were perfectly shaped, and her shapely legs were long and slender and led to her French manicured toes, which matched her fingers. I would never have imagined this was the body of Carolyn Autumn. She was so darn conservative and conscientious all the time. *Damn shame*, I thought to myself.

"Adam," Mrs. Autumn called from her chair, motioning me to come over to the table. I went over to her and she covered the phone with her free hand and whispered for me to have a seat. I pulled out a chair and sat down. Mrs. Autumn's conversation was obviously personal in nature although she made no effort to keep it private. She was telling the person on the other end how she could care less how he spent his money anymore as long as she got a check every month. I knew she was talking about her estranged husband. The whole neighborhood knew they were getting a divorce, if they hadn't already, and that it was getting ugly. She belittled the man vehemently every chance she could get. I wondered how this made Carolyn feel. After-all, he was still her father who she saw on a regular basis. Carolyn's father did everything he could to make Carolyn happy. Since the divorce he had done his best to spend time with Carolyn and talk to her every day on the phone. Carolyn's Mom and Dad knew my parents and trusted them.

After about five awkward minutes of sitting next to Mrs. Autumn while she finished her conversation, she hung up. She wore a bright orange bikini and sunglasses with a little silver butterfly on each frame. Expensive is one way of describing her, forward would have been another. Everything about her was always scrupulously in place and classy. I never saw Mrs. Autumn when she didn't look ready to attend a formal event at a moment's notice. High maintenance and probably not a very good cook was how my father once described her. John said she was a classic MILF and I totally agreed.

It felt odd to be looking at Mrs. Autumn in her bra and panties, or bikini as the case may have been. Well, that is essentially what a bikini is after-all. She looked perfect as always and I couldn't help wondering that Carolyn must get it from her mother; her constant drive to be perfect in school. Carolyn was always nicely dressed, but not to the extent Mrs. Autumn was. Mrs. Autumn dressed sexy nice; Carolyn dressed conservative nice.

Carolyn wasn't as materialistic either. She didn't care if she was wearing a pair of designer sunglasses or not, as long as they blocked the sun. With her mother being so lavish and flashy, she had probably had enough of it and wanted to just blend in. Carolyn's subtleness made her more appealing and somewhat mysterious in the sense that you didn't know what was underneath - at least not until now. After having known Carolyn my whole life and never giving her any thought, I realized how people can change, and seemingly overnight at that.

Mrs. Autumn pushed her sunglasses up onto the top of her head as she leaned back in her chair. "It's a hot one," she said, fanning herself. "Are you going to work in this heat?"

"Sure," I shrugged. "It's not that bad."

It was about ninety degrees. I could tell Mrs. Autumn was hot; there were beads of sweat on her chest. Even the sweat on Mrs. Autumn looked perfect, as though a photographer had sprayed water on her chest to make it glisten for the camera. Although I always knew Mrs. Autumn was very attractive, I had never seen her like this before and felt somewhat guilty for my thoughts. She was Carolyn's mom and about forty. They had kids at a young age. Young to be Carolyn's mother for sure, but for my age, that was old. I never checked out forty-year-old women--they were just out of my range.

"I have plenty of work to keep you busy. It's just Carolyn and me here now. As you can tell, we're not much good at yard work," she said with a knowing smirk. I pictured Carolyn and Mrs. Autumn in the back yard in their bikinis trying to remove stumps and I returned the smile. "As far as pay," she said, "what is your rate?"

"Ten an hour," I said.

"Fine, you keep track of your time. Like I said, there's plenty to do. You'll be well worth it. I had to go and hire someone to come and take care of the pool. It costs forty bucks every time that guy comes and pours stuff in the pool. You can handle that as well?" she stated more than asked.

"What do I have to do?"

"I don't know. I've never done it. Carolyn claims she knows, but I don't want her handling all those chemicals. All the bottles have warnings on them and the last thing I need is for her to go splashing it in her eye or something."

"No problem," I laughed, knowing I could find out how to do just about anything on the Internet.

"The backyard's a mess. I had three trees removed last year and the guy who took them down didn't remove the stumps. They're big ones too. The yard needs to be mowed every week, the bushes need to be trimmed, we need more mulch around the whole place, and we need everything weeded. You can start on that." Mrs.

Autumn got up and tied a white wrap around her waist. I followed her past the pool and into their large yard, her hips swaying hypnotically with each step she took. As we walked I caught wafts of, what I thought was, the scent of Mrs. Autumn's body. In reality though, it was probably a mixture of shampoo, conditioner and body lotion. "Beautiful trees. Fucking Dutch Elms disease," she said, and then looked at me smiling. "You will excuse my language, won't you, Adam?" I didn't answer her quickly enough. I was still inhaling deeply through my nose to finish smelling the breeze she left while walking.

"The heat getting to you already?" she asked. "You haven't even started working yet."

"No. I was just looking at the stumps. Sorry." She wasn't kidding. The three stumps were huge. They had been big trees.

"Damn beetles spread the disease. Originated in Asia and then spread to Europe and America. The things you can learn from a tree trimmer, huh? Guy wanted to talk my ear off."

"Wow," I said. I pictured the tree trimmer pontificating like an arborist while addressing Mrs. Autumn's breasts. She pointed out the shed in the back corner of the yard. Mr. Autumn (Chuck) had left every tool known to man, including a chainsaw, which I was relieved to find. They also had a riding lawn mower. *This was going to be fun work*, I thought. What guy didn't like to ride around on a lawn mower and play with a chainsaw? I would have to keep quiet about the chainsaw, though. If my father knew I was using one he would think I was going to cut off a limb.

"Thanks for helping out, Adam. It's good to have someone you know doing the work," Mrs. Autumn said before heading back to her chair on the patio for another phone conversation. I tried to catch her scent again by walking to the spot where she previously stood, but missed it. I figured out how I was going to attack the stumps. If I dug a deep trench around each stump I would be able to use the chainsaw to cut the stump out below the surface of the ground. I could then fill the void with soil and plant grass seed. The stumps were a nuisance, an obstacle to avoid while mowing. I gathered the tools I needed from the shed. It was very hot in the shed, at least ten degrees hotter than outside. I then began to work on the first stump.

After about an hour of digging on the first day, I was already beat. The stumps were going to be a real pain in the ass. I worked for four hours and only completed the trench around two stumps. Carolyn and her mom were out at the pool the whole time. They laid on the lawn chairs until the heat became too much for them, then one of them would jump in the pool and swim around for a few minutes. Mrs. Autumn was frequently on the phone. I decided to call it a day. Working out in an air conditioned gym is one thing, but manual labor is another altogether. I wasn't used to this kind of work. My hands were sore and blistering from using the shovel and my back ached. I should have looked for some gardening gloves in that shed before I started. I tried not to show any signs of being tired in front of the Autumn ladies. One needs to protect ones reputation at all costs.

CHAPTER FIVE

Fishing with Friends

B EHIND OUR HOUSES WAS A nice sized pond. Beyond that was a forest preserve with paths people used for hiking or biking. The pond had a gazebo placed on a concrete slab about thirty feet out into the water. A wooden boardwalk led from the shore to the gazebo. It was the kind of boardwalk where you heard footsteps echoing in the space between the boards and the water. This spot, although picture perfect, was seldom used. You had to traverse several paths and travel quite a distance from the entrance of the forest preserve to get to it. It was not easy to locate by going through the forest preserve, but from our backyards we could make it to the gazebo along the bank of the pond in only fifteen minutes.

This was where Mark, Joey, and I went fishing. When the sun started to go down, I called the guys. I had made sure I bought my favorite lure, the Mr. Champ. It was a spoon lure, small but very heavy and I loved casting it. We hiked out to the gazebo, settled in, and started casting. We all liked to fish, but Mark was really into it. At least more into it than Joey or me. He had a different pole for every different kind of fish. He had a bass rod, a northern rod, one for crappie and one for carp and catfish. He even had a saltwater spin rod. I don't think Mark had ever even seen the ocean. His lure collection was enormous. Deep divers, rattle traps, top water baits, jigs, and spoons. He would pull out a huge wooden lure about a foot long and point out little scratches he described as teeth marks. There would be some story about the enormous fish he caught on it to follow.

I had been going fishing with Mark since we were little kids. In fact the only time Mark ever went fishing that I knew of was with me or Joey, and we barely ever caught anything. He would go on and on about the musky or northern he had caught on a fishing trip to Canada or the deep north woods. I never remembered Mark ever leaving the state. Mark's father was, in fact, a real outdoorsman though. He had shotguns displayed in glass cases throughout the house. He had a mounted black bear in the basement and deer pelts on the floors. He went hunting and brought home deer venison steaks and jerky. The jerky was quite good. Mark's father never took him along and Mark never spoke about that, and I never asked. Mark's father wasn't someone you wanted to mess with. He was a big strong man, over six feet tall. "Hardened from all the years working construction," my father would say. "Shaking hands with Dick Bogan feels like you're holding a brick!" When Mark, Joey, and I snuck out in the middle of the night, we never met at Mark's house. We knew if Mark's dad thought someone was trying to break in we might get shot. His friends called him 'Big' Dick Bogan.

My family took a vacation every summer to Millinocket, Maine, where we stayed at the same cabin every year. Millinocket was where my mother used to go with her father when she was young. My mom's mother had passed away when she was nine. She had fond memories of Millinocket, and Dad made sure she got there every year. We went there for our "peace of Maine," Dad said. The lake was just a short walk from the cabin and, every year, armed with our nearly disposable Zebco, gas station variety rod and reel combos and a plastic container of wax worms, we would fail at fishing. The fishing there was said to be outstanding, but we could never figure out how to catch anything. Dad would say, "They're not biting today, guys. I bet there's a warm front coming in." My brother and I thought he knew what he was talking about, but now we know better. Every time the fish didn't bite it was blamed on a warm front, whether or not there was actually a warm front. Mark argued that fishing during a warm front was the best time to fish. I no longer cared. I just enjoyed being outside casting into the water. Catching the fish was a bonus.

We arrived at the gazebo at what we called prime time; the time of day when the sun was just starting to go down. From prime time until dark was the best time to catch fish. The early morning was another period of prime time, but we were all too lazy to get up that early. We began fishing and, as customary, the fish didn't bite, not even a nibble. It was a hot day so I figured the fish had moved off to deeper areas of the lake to avoid swimming in, what could be considered, the bath temperature water where we were casting. After an hour or so, and none of us getting as much as a nibble, I moved on to a more entertaining activity: annoying Mark.

"I bet I can cast further than you," I baited him.

"In your dreams," he said with a laugh.

"Ask Joey," I said. "He knows who the real sportsman is."

"Totally!" Joey chimed in.

"Dude, I've been fishing my whole life. Just don't start. Do you know how much gear I have? That's what I do all summer, dude. You're so stupid," he said, starting to get irritated.

"I'm the real deal, dude. I'm the fucking sportsman," I said. Mark shook his head and his face reddened.

"God! You people are so stupid! I'm a friggin' pro. I grew up fishing, dude!"

"I'm the real deal, that's all I'm saying."

"You're ignorant, is what you are. Do you know how much gear I have? I'm a sportsman. I spend my summers in the north fucking woods, man. That's what I do!"

"Then let's have a cast-off, bitch!" I said prodding him further.

"OOH A CAST OFF!" Joey hollered, laughing at Mark.

"God! You're so stupid!" he said "Fine. Let me set up a rig then. I'm friggin using an ultra-lite here." Mark had three poles with him. He switched his pole and tied on a heavy yellow jig he thought would cast farthest. "Dude, you know you can't beat me," Mark said. "I've been doing this my whole life! I'm a friggin outdoorsman."

We set up the rules. We would each have three casts, best out of three. Joey would be the judge and I would go first. I got my pole ready for the cast of its life. I let the lure hang below the rod tip with about a foot and a half of line so I could get a good sling shot action happening. I deftly flung the pole behind me and then swung it forward as fast and as hard as I could yelling, "Mr. Champ!" The line snapped taut and I realized that in my excitement the bail had slipped closed during my cast and I snagged something good. I had set the hook perfectly in Mark's upper lip. Two prongs of the Mr. Champ had cleanly pierced through the fatty tissue which was bleeding in a fast, consistent drip.

"You fucking affhole!" Mark mumbled while he drooled and bled on the wooden gazebo floor. I ran to Mark's backpack to try and find something for him to put on his mouth to stop the bleeding, or at least catch the constant drip of blood that was getting all over his clothes. The backpack only contained the essentials. A box of lures, needle nose pliers, and a bag of those god-damned potato chips.

CHAPTER SIX

A Visit to the Hospital

I ACCOMPANIED MARK AND HIS MOTHER to the emergency room. After-all it was my fault.

"You're no sportsman!" Mark told me while sitting in the small room, waiting for the doctor to return. I put my hand on Mark's shoulder.

"I'm sorry, man. I didn't…"

"Just stop," he interrupted, shrugging my hand off. And there we sat in uncomfortable silence. Mark wouldn't even look at me. Mrs. Bogan was always really nice to me and I liked her, but I felt awful sitting there with her, knowing it was all my fault. I didn't mean to hook Mark in the lip, Mark was my best friend.

"Mark Bogan?" the emergency room nurse called out.

Both Mrs. Bogan and I stood up with Mark. Mark turned and looked at us and mumbled through his bloody towel, "I don't need any friggin help." He followed the nurse through the double doors and out of sight. Mrs. Bogan and I sat back down and watched the door close behind him.

It was always a little awkward being around Mrs. Bogan. Joey and I had made so many jokes about her, and I had an unfounded paranoia that she knew about it. Mark's mom wasn't particularly attractive but she did have big breasts. Breasts that weren't that big a few years ago. *Shit!* I thought. *Here I am in the emergency room with Mark and his mother, all because of me, and I am staring at his mom's tits.* I lifted my gaze from Mrs. Bogan's breasts to her face. Our eyes met and she winked at me. I quickly glanced at the table next to me and started rifling through the magazines. I picked up a *Readers Digest* and started reading an article. I didn't understand anything I was reading. I was in shock. I thought about how Mark said the women in the neighborhood were in heat and going through a mid-life crisis. Was Mrs. Bogan in heat? She'd possibly spent too much time with Mrs. Autumn.

I thought about Mark and the lure in his lip. I had fond memories of the Mr. Champ lure. It was my favorite and I used it just about every time we went fishing. I had first found it at the gas station that doubled as the local bait shop in Millinocket. When I was younger, it was the most appealing lure because it was the shiniest. It was also the heaviest, so it could cast the farthest. If you weren't catching fish, seeing how far you could cast was just as much fun. While waiting for Mark to come out, I thought about how I would now have mixed feelings about the Mr. Champ. It would always remind me of Millinocket, but how could I ever forget it dangling from Mark's lip with blood dripping from the end of it?

After about fifteen minutes the doctor came out. He explained to us that two of the barbs on the treble hook had completely pierced Mark's philtrum (upper lip) and narrowly avoided his vermillion border, the area where the lip meets the face. This, he assured us, was good news since the hook could be removed with minimal surgical intervention through the sting and yank method. It would require the administration of local anesthetic. The sting and yank method was simply pushing the hook down into the skin so that when you yanked the hook out the barbs would not cause any new trauma to the skin. They would also grind down the barbs on the treble hook to minimize any further trauma. Mrs. Bogan thanked the doctor for the update and he disappeared to complete the procedure. The whole explanation made me cringe and my own lips tingled in sympathy for Mark.

Mark's upper lip only looked bad for a couple of days; fat as a hot dog. He refused to leave the house until the swelling went down. For four days I went to Mark's and hung out with him. I really did feel bad about the whole thing. He was always watching some action or adventure movie, something like *Raiders of the Lost Ark* or *Die Hard*. I apologized to Mark several times for hooking his lip. One time he even explained it wasn't really my fault. He told me that the problem was that I didn't have enough experience casting. I let it go. After-all I did mess up the cast, and after snagging Mark like a spawning carp I guess I deserved a little abuse.

Mark's parents weren't doing well. He opened up to me more than usual about it during one of my recovery visits. It was really bugging him. They didn't want to talk to him about it, so he talked to me about it instead. I felt strange talking to Mark about his parents fighting, but I knew he needed to get it off his chest. My parents were doing great. I felt bad that things were going so well for my family while his was falling apart.

"It's like when these woman around here hit a certain age they go fucking nuts, man," Mark said. "They friggin have everything they could ever want. A nice house, a great car, a family. I just don't get it. And another thing, that Mrs. Autumn isn't helping things. My mom is on the phone with her all the damn time. I know she is egging my mom on. I overhear their conversations all the time."

"What's Mrs. Autumn telling her?" I asked.

"I'm not sure exactly what she's saying. I just know

that after she gets off the phone with that bitch my parents fight like cats and dogs. All these women are in heat!"

"Just give it some time man. They'll work it out," I reasoned.

"That's what I'm afraid of. They're going to work themselves right out of their marriage." It wasn't just Mark's mom either. I knew other woman in the neighborhood who chummed around with Mrs. Autumn. I saw them at the popular local restaurants that offered an upbeat atmosphere and cocktails. "This town is full of meat markets!" my dad said whenever we walked into one of the local restaurants where the bar was packed with middle-aged woman, who were either divorced, or in the process of pursuing younger men. "A bunch of restless hens." My father called them.

The amusing thing was once these women divorced they left their nice big homes and ended up in little apartments or condos. You could see the change in lifestyle by the cars they drove as well. No longer were they driving the nice Mercedes or BMW. It was a Toyota Camry or a Volkswagen Jetta now. The men always disappeared after the divorce. You never saw them anymore. It's like they wanted to get away from the women, the town, and the memory of it. Something I would come to understand.

Walking home that night from Mark's through our

seemingly perfect little neighborhood, I felt uneasy. I came to the realization that inside these homes that looked so nice on the outside, the people inside were living frantic lives of desperation. Not knowing exactly what they wanted, just that it wasn't what they already had. At least, not at that moment. Being raised Catholic, I didn't understand why people couldn't just make marriage work. After-all, once you got married you couldn't get divorced, no matter what. It was a sin. Whatever your differences, you just had to work them out. That was all there was to. Well, that's how it worked in my family anyway.

The next morning I woke up at ten. I quickly ate some waffles and hit the gym with Mark and Joey. We were all using the same bench press that morning and took turns. We were in no hurry.

"Man, last night Christine came by for a few hours," Mark said.

"Yeah?" I asked. "You guys mess around?"

"Oh yeah," he said.

"Dude, you gotta tell me what happened," Joey said.

Mark finished his set and sat up. "My friggin mom walked in on us!" Mark said.

"WHAT?" Joey asked loudly.

"Yeah dude. I'm on the couch with her in the basement. We're watching *Die Hard* and…"

"You were watching *Die Hard*?" I interrupted. "You fucking just watched that the other day"

"Dude, girls like action movies. It gets them hot!" Mark argued.

"Go on man, what happened next?" Joey pleaded.

"When chicks see guys kicking ass like Bruce Willis does in that movie they get all turned on and shit. Trust me, man! It's damn near fool proof."

I sighed. "Just go on."

"Whatever dude, chicks friggin like that shit. It's like a pheromone or something. So we're on the couch. She's getting all hot from the movie or whatever and we're going at it pretty good. I'm on top straddling her and then she starts going for my shirt."

"Oh man!" Joey cried.

"But dude, I'm kinda freaking out at this point. See, I have this huge boner. And it's so big that it's poking out of the top of my pants about an inch and a half! Now the angle I'm sitting on her is crazy. If she pulls my shirt up or off, my boner is going to be right in her face!"

"OH DUDE!" Joey yelled while jumping around.

"What the hell is your dick doing all the way up there, hanging out of the top of your pants?" I asked.

"What do you mean?"

"Well, why was your penis pointing straight up and out of your pants?"

"Dude, that's how all penises bend, straight up. You know, towards your chest," Mark assured me.

"What?" I asked. "My penis doesn't bend up like that. Dude, when I get a boner I point it down my leg... not up my pants toward my damn belly button!"

"That's not normal!" Mark said.

"Joey, does your dick bow up or down?" I asked.

"My dick's just like Mark's, dude," Joey said a little too loudly. The guy at the squat machine was looking over at us. Now I was freaked and didn't want to talk about the way my penis bowed anymore.

"Just finish the gawd damned story" I said.

"That's fucking odd, dude, you should get checked out," Mark said, and then continued. "So I don't want to freak her out or anything with my boner like right in her face, but at the same time, this is like the perfect situation for a blow job. She starts to go for my shirt so I decide to hug her. That way she will be able to feel my boner on her chest and if she wants to give me a B.J., she can, but at least she knows it's right there. Well this didn't turn out to be the right move either, cause as soon as I started hugging her I got so worked up, I started to cum."

"Oh come on" I said. "Are you kidding me?"

"No dude, we had been grinding for like ever!"

"Oh my gawd!" Joey said.

"Yeah, yeah, I know. But it gets worse. I don't want her to know what just happened, you know? But right after I'm done my mom walks in the room. So I jump off her, my mom's standing there in the doorway trying to talk to me and I'm still facing Christine. I look down, and I'm covered in my own mess and Christine's looking right at it."

"Did your mom see it?" Joey asked.

"No. That's the good thing. She wanted help bringing up a laundry basket and I told her I would come help her in a minute. She knew something was going on though because she talked to me later about not closing the door when I was with Christine."

All I could do was shake my head.

The rest of the day and into the night I worried constantly that something might be wrong with my wiener. Previously, I was only concerned that my penis was small. I had watched porno movies before and my penis was nowhere near as large as the ones I saw in those movies. I kept imagining the poor girl who would finally be gracious enough to pull my penis out of my pants. She would take one look and say, "Oh my gawd! What is wrong with it? It's so small, and it's bent all funny!"

Then she would run out of the room. So after six or seven hours of scenarios such as this playing over and over in my head I decided to have the awkward conversation with my mother. I chose my mother simply because if my father thought there may be something wrong with my wiener I would be at Dr. Jake's office first thing in the morning. I didn't want Dr. Jakes feeling me up. Upon returning home from hanging out at Mark's with Joey, I found my mother alone in her office.

"Mom," I said, sitting down.

"Hey Adam, how's it going?" she said turning her leather swivel chair away from her computer to face me.

"Ahh okay," I said, obviously in a way that indicated I was not in fact okay. She could tell instantly I was concerned about something.

"What's wrong, honey?" she asked. I didn't want to explain that I was with my friends talking about our cocks so I concocted a story.

"Well, I was kind of concerned about something. I had a health teacher that told us that a guy's penis is supposed to point straight up when he has an erection. Like up straight along your belly. I was just kind of worried because that's not exactly how it is for me."

"What does yours do?" she asked very simply.

"It just sticks straight out. But not straight up towards the ceiling!"

"Adam, you are built just the way you should be. I have changed your diapers enough times to know that!" she smiled. "Every man I have ever been with was built the same exact way you are." This new information was a huge relief to me. All of it besides the thought that every man my mother had slept with or fooled around with had a cock that stuck out perpendicularly and not vertically. Some things you just wish you didn't know.

"Well that's what I thought too! But the teacher kept saying it should stick straight up."

My mother just smiled at me assuredly. "You're just fine."

Armed with this reassuring new information I went up to my bedroom. I planned to head over to the Autumn's house in the morning. I stripped down to my boxer shorts and climbed into bed. I was tired. My constant worrying about my penis during the day had exhausted me. I turned the CD player on my nightstand on and listened to *Dreams* by Fleetwood Mac. Moments later I was asleep.

CHAPTER SEVEN

Back to Work

U PON ARRIVING AT THE AUTUMN'S house I was pleasantly surprised to find Carolyn lying in the backyard on a lawn chair again. She was in a pink bikini this time. I didn't fail to notice how good the bright colored material made her tan look.

"Hey Carolyn," I said, trying not to stare.

"Fine. I mean how are you? I'm fine," she said, eventually figuring it out.

"Good," I said with a smile. "What you up to this summer? Anything exciting?" I asked.

"Not much. I have nothing planned. How about you?"

"I don't have anything going on either," I said. "Just doing some work on the side. Keep the parents happy, you know."

"Yeah. Well I'm glad you're here. The pool is starting to grow green stuff in it," she laughed.

"Oh yeah, that's all me, isn't it?" I said inspecting the algae that was beginning to attach to the sides of the pool.

"Yup, you know what to do?"

"No friggin' clue."

She got up and told me to follow her. As I followed, I performed my usual hot chick routine. I sniffed the air she left behind as she walked, her jet stream so to speak. She smelled great, a mix of something fruity and sun tan oil. She actually smelled better than Mrs. Autumn; younger and less floral. We arrived at the shed in the corner of the huge backyard where she opened the door and stepped in. I followed close behind, or as close behind as I could without weirding her out. It was a large shed but packed with stuff. Shovels for the winter, a snow blower, the riding lawn mower, pool filters, decorations for the front lawn for all the holidays, old pool toys from when Carolyn was little, etc.

"The stuff is somewhere back here. The guy that my mom hired to do the chemicals brought his own," she said as she squeezed into the back of the shed between a set of shelves. I followed her through the dusty shed and stood next to her. It was hot as hell in the shed and it smelled like lumber, grass clippings, dust, and Carolyn. I focused in on the scent of her. We were standing very close, almost touching, I could feel the heat radiating off our bodies and oddly, I felt as though the body heat was communicating back and forth between us. This sensation was so strong and unusual, that I turned away from the shelf and stared at her. To my surprise she turned to face me and gazed directly into my eyes.

"Adam?" she asked putting her index finger into her mouth and touching her tongue.

"Yes?"

"You have something in your ear." She reached out and put her wet finger in my ear.

"Wow. Seriously? You know you just started a war, don't you?"

"If you say so," she said, grinning up at me before turning back toward the shelf.

"Here it is," she said, pointing to a big box up on the shelf. I reached out and pulled it down. Inside were white puck-like chlorine tabs and several gallon containers of other chemicals.

"My dad used to just keep these chorine tabs in the pool all the time. As long as they are in there, he never worried about any of the chemical levels."

"That sounds easy enough." She turned to leave the shed and I followed her through the yard back to the patio. When we got back to her chair she sat down, smiled and said, "I thought your ball must have rolled back here when you came over yesterday."

"Except I don't play with balls anymore," I said.

"That's doubtful," she said looking down towards my crotch.

"Funny. But no kidding. We haven't hung out since we were little, huh?" I said stuffing several of the chlorine tabs into a floating frog.

"Yeah, well, Mark and Joey probably have more in common with you than I do," she said.

"I think you're cool though. I would hang out with you." I threw the frog into the pool and watched it splash.

"Even after I told on you for jumping out the back of the bus?"

"That was you, wasn't it? Maybe I need to think about this again." I smiled. "You had to study, wasn't it?"

"Oh my gawd, stop. It was a long time ago!" she said covering her face with her hands, laughing. I sat down on the chair next to her.

"I forgive you," I said. She looked up, a serious expression taking over her features.

"I didn't apologize, did I?"

"Oh you're a tough one."

"I do want to apologize though. Not for telling on the bus, but for the way my mom was acting the other day."

"What? Don't be silly," I said.

"No really. It's bad enough that she talks about him like that in private, but in front of my... well... friends," she smiled, "that's just plain wrong and I'm sorry you had to hear it."

"Don't worry about it. Honestly. Parents can be really embarrassing. I know. Have you ever heard my Dad sing at church? Or crochet in front of my friends?"

I worked in the Autumn's yard for several more hours that day. I was able to completely remove two of the stumps. In between working on the stumps I stopped by to visit Carolyn who alternated between laying out and swimming around the pool, just the same as last time. The radio was on and playing the soundtrack to the summer. Many of the songs that played that summer would stay with me forever as a reminder of those days.

Carolyn and I were alone. I loved just being able to come back and forth and talk with her here and there. I was doing my best to be interesting, funny and charming. I suppose you could've called it flirting. Just being polite and friendly was the only way I knew of flirting. I had seen Mark flirt before, it was scummy. Like a dirty old man staring inappropriately at a poor girl and saying something raunchy and disgusting. I couldn't figure out if Carolyn was flirting too. Was she always this damn cute? Were her mannerisms always so sexy and, at least to me, seductive, or was she also flirting? I looked forward to coming back to her house and working. My mind was set. I wanted Carolyn. Although I had gotten a few other calls from neighbors who wanted me to mow their lawns, I wouldn't be calling them back.

CHAPTER EIGHT

A Standard Night

AFTER WORKING OVER AT CAROLYN'S house for most of the day I came home, cleaned up, and called up Mark and Joey. We all wanted to do something that night so everyone came over to my house and we sat on the back patio trying to figure out something to do. Lots of times during the summer we would snipe some beer from Mark's dad. Mr. Bogan had a bar set up down in his finished basement and he had beer on tap. We would take empty two liter bottles and fill them up, put them in our backpacks and sit on the gazebo, passing them around. We would sit there until late at night listening to the chirp of crickets and the croak of toads. Unfortunately Mr. Bogan's keg was dry, so we couldn't snatch any from him. I wasn't sure Mark was ready to visit the gazebo again just yet. I was sure his blood would still be all over the floor. Joey's parents didn't drink and my parent's alcohol stash was so small I would exhaust it in the matter of a few months if I dipped into it every weekend.

The patio door opened and John came bounding out with his friend Stokes. I'm not sure what Stokes' first name was, I don't think I ever heard it used.

"What's up, douche bag?" John asked me. "Ladies," he said, addressing Mark and Joey. I just rolled my eyes and kept my mouth shut.

"Hey John, how about getting us some brewskies?" Mark said. John and Stokes looked at each other and burst into laughter

"Brewskies eh?" John said. "You're a fucking tool!" Mark always tried to act cool in front of John.

"Yeah dude, can you get us some beers?" Mark continued.

"What's in it for me, dude?" John asked.

"You buy us a twelver and we buy you a twelver?" Mark offered.

"Fine. Give me the money and we'll be back in a bit."

"No way. We're coming with you. Last time I gave you money to buy me cigars you never came back and I never got my money back."

"Fine dude, let them come with," Stokes said. "We need the twelver for tonight anyway."

"Okay assholes. You can come with but I don't want

you queers sucking each other's cocks in my back seat. You got it?" We just ignored him.

"You got it?" John demanded.

"Yeah, dude," Joey said.

"I need each of you to promise me you won't suck each other off in my back seat on the way there." Mark tried to explain he wasn't gay and that he gets tons of pussy to prove it.

"Each of you needs to promise me you won't do it before we leave."

"Fine," I said, knowing this could go on all night. "I won't suck anyone's cock on the way there."

"That's not gonna do it, Adam," John said. "I need you to promise Joey and Mark here individually that you won't try and suck *their* cocks on the way to the liquor store."

"You're such an asshole, dude," I said, earning myself a punch in the arm. It hurt too.

"Fine. Mark, I won't try and suck your dick in the back seat on the way to buy beer. Joey, I won't try and suck your dick on the way to the store to buy beer. There. Are you happy now?" Mark and Joey had to give the same promises before we could leave. Joey seemed to even enjoy it. He thought it was funny as hell. Mark and I couldn't stand it.

We climbed into the back of John's mini-van. He

hated the mini-van but my parents gave it to him to take to college so he couldn't complain too much. He got a car for free for frig's sake. We had to drive a few towns over to a store that would sell to John with his fake ID. The liquor store was in a large strip mall. Once we got there John drove around the large parking lot about five times harassing people. John would pull up to someone just coming out of a store.

"Excuse me. Do you know what time it is?" Stokes asked. Just as the person looked down to try and access his watch, John took off and left the person standing there confused. It was pretty funny the first few time, but after the fifth time it started to get old. Not to Joey though. He just laughed and laughed. At times he was laughing so hard he could hardly breathe. Mark and I just wanted to get the beer and get home.

We got a twelve pack of Budweiser and unpacked it into the backpack I had brought along. When we got back to our neighborhood we had John drop us off several houses away from Mark's. From there we walked along the pond to a clearing deep in the forest where we had cleared out a little spot years go. We had a metal pail half buried in the forest debris and three plastic buckets surrounding it. This was our little bonfire pit. Underneath our buckets we each kept contraband in gallon sized freezer bags. Under mine were two packs of cigarettes, one Marlboro, one Newport, and a flask-sized bottle of peppermint schnapps. Joey had a *Hustler* magazine and a tin of Skoal Longcut. Mark had half a plastic Gatorade bottle of Crown Royal and a huge bag of unopened au gratin potato chips. The chips weren't there last time. I eyed Mark, wondering when he'd brought the chips there on his own.

We walked around and picked up a few armfuls of twigs and then larger branches to keep our small fire going. I got it going easily after only a few matches and we sat down around the small blazing bucket.

"Now this is the life," Mark said as he cracked open a Budweiser.

"Hell yeah," Joey responded. Mark ripped open his fresh bag of potato chips and placed a large chip precisely in his mouth. Joey looked at me and started laughing in his goofy obnoxious way. I just shook my head.

"What the fuck, dude?" Mark asked. "What's your problem?"

"Nothing, dude!" Joey said, still red faced and laughing.

"Just forget about it, Mark," I said, trying to avoid a fight and messing up the night.

"I'm sick of this shit. Why do you have to start? What the fuck is your problem? Am I bothering you? I didn't eat dinner, dude. I'm hungry. So fucking what?" Mark hollered.

"Dude! You fucking snuck back here to hide potato chips!" Joey blurted out, still laughing.

"Joey, he didn't hide them back here, man. He's hungry. Just leave him alone," I reasoned. Joey just started laughing even harder. Then tried to hold it back, snorting the harder he tried. Mark was staring off into the trees.

"Okay. Okay, I'm sorry. I just think it's weird, man, that's all," Joey said.

"Mark, it's cool man," I said. "I fucking jerk off like three times a day sometimes. We all have our shit we do, man. We all have shit." Mark looked over at me.

"Fucking three times a day, dude? Are you serious? That's got to be some kind of record!"

"Not for me it's not," I replied under my breath. "Fuck it, man. Let's just chill out and enjoy these brews."

"Deal," Mark said.

"Deal," Joey said.

"Deal," I chimed in. "I'm doing work over at the Autumn's house this summer," I told them. "It's been pretty cool so far."

"Working for that bitch? Man I don't like her, dude," Mark said.

"She is so damn hot though!" Joey said.

"Yeah, she's smoking, but Autumn's a god-damned home wrecker. Fucking bitch is in heat," Mark said.

"I saw her in her bikini the other day, dude. Bra and panties," I said. Mark raised his beer up in the air.

"Here, here," he said and we all toasted each other.

"You know Carolyn is a pretty cool chick," I said, testing the waters.

"She's a DORK," Joey said.

"She's actually pretty cool. I was talking to her the other day. I kind of dig her."

"You've always had a crush on that ding bat haven't you?" Mark asked.

"Yeah bro, I think I kind of like her the way you like your fucking au gratins," I said while staring into the fire. Mark looked over at me for a second, then turned back towards the fire and shook his head.

"What prospects do you have over there, loud mouth?" I asked Joey.

"Dude, I'm working on this one chick at church," he said. Joey's family was Christian. Mark and I were Christian too, but we were Catholic--very traditional. I went to Joey's church once and it was not what I was used to. They had a band on stage. Electric guitar, drums, the whole nine yards. People were dancing around and shit too. It made me feel uncomfortable as hell.

"What's her name? Where does she go to school? Why haven't I heard you talk about her?" I asked.

"I don't know dude," Joey said in his usual overly excited, overly loud way.

"What's the mark's name, dude?" Mark asked. A "mark" is a term we used to describe someone or something we were after. Marks were like targets.

"Don't call her a mark," Joey said. "Her name is Bridget. She's a year younger than us."

"Awfully touchy about some chicklet we've never even heard you mention before, aren't you?"

"I just think she's cool. That's all," Joey admitted.

"Where's the mystery girl go to school?" Mark asked again. Joey was avoiding eye contact.

"She's home schooled." Mark and I both stared at Joey.

"You got to be fucking kidding me?" Mark said.

"Just stop. Don't fucking start, will you?" Joey said.

"Joey, hold on. You're serious? You're gonna drop a fucking bomb like that on us and you don't think you're gonna take shit for it?" I asked.

"If you guys were fucking cool you would just drop it, that's all I'm saying. It's fucking nothing, man. She's home schooled. So what?"

"Joey! Look at Jerry Bleaker, that's what home schooling does," Mark said.

"Jerry Bleaker is a fucking nerd. In all the years we've grown up here we hardly ever see him. He never leaves the house!" Joey protested.

"Right, that's because he's home schooled," Mark said. Joey pulled three beers out of the backpack.

"Let's shotgun, pussies," he said attempting to change the conversation. It worked. We shot gunned the beers, smoked some cigarettes and relaxed in one of the most perfect settings you could ask for. We were good friends, and we had a great time together that night just talking and enjoying the intermittent silences filled with the sound of the forest. The thing that made it extra special for me was the thought of Carolyn, the butterflies in my stomach, and the anticipation of seeing her the next day.

CHAPTER NINE

More Uncomfortable Moments

I WOKE UP LATER THAN USUAL the next morning. I got out of bed at ten feeling not so great. It was probably from shot gunning the beers the night before. My dad was still complaining about Mr. Berry's dog Scooter when I went down for breakfast.

"It's not that big a deal," I told him.

"It is a big deal, Adam. There's residue all over this backyard," he said while gazing out the window. Telling my father not to let things bother him so much was ironic. I was the master at letting things get to me.

I wasted no time getting a move on and heading to Carolyn's house. On my short walk I wondered if she would be wearing a different bikini. So far she had worn a different one each day, first white, then pink. The memory of what happened in the shed kept replaying over in my head. Being that close to her had exhilarated me beyond words. Her playful wet-willy had tantalized me. As I walked, my stomach began to feel like I was swinging high on a swing, leaving it behind as I swung back down from a height, short of breath. Then doubt and negativity decided to pay a visit. I worried that she was just being friendly and cordial towards me. After all, she was very well mannered. Maybe she hadn't been flirting at all. It was quite possible that her eyes always shined when she smiled. Perhaps I had just missed it in the past because I never saw her as anyone interesting. I hadn't paid much attention to her in school or on the bus. She never stood out with her understated dress and shyness. She was changing from how she had been. She was growing up.

I spotted her lying out on a lawn chair again as I came around the side of the house and into the backyard. She did have a different bikini on, just as I had suspected. This time it was red and it looked just as good as the pink one had. She was lying face down on the lawn chair so she hadn't noticed me just yet. I looked down at my clothes and felt somewhat self-conscious. She looked amazing and I was wearing thin nylon workout pants and a Budweiser t-shirt. I ducked back around the side of the house before she had the chance to hear me coming. I figured I could impress her a little bit if I took off my shirt. I got down on the ground and started pumping out push-ups. I did fifty in a row as fast as I could, looking around self- consciously as I did them and praying no one would see me. I looked like an asshole and felt like one too. I sprung up and let the pump set in. Once I felt I was sufficiently pumped up I swaggered into the backyard and announced, "Hey Sexy!" thinking this greeting would put a smile on Carolyn's face, if not make her laugh.

The girl on the chair slowly raised herself up onto her elbows and turned to face me. I quickly realized two things. First, she wasn't wearing her bikini top. It was unfastened and lying on the chair underneath her. Second, and to my complete horror, the girl was not Carolyn. It was her mom.

"Adam?" Mrs. Autumn said as she focused on me. I was staring at her tits with my mouth hanging wide open. She had turned to lie on her side and propped her head up with her right hand. On her face she wore a mischievous smirk.

"Oh fuck. I mean I was joking. It was a joke. I mean, I meant to say that to Carolyn, but as a joke you know, as a joke," I said.

"Do I look offended Adam?"

"No, or, I'm not sure. I didn't know it was, well I didn't know," I said, still gawking at her breasts, seemingly unable to drag my eyeballs away from them.

"You don't have to explain yourself. It would take a

lot more than that to offend me. In fact, Adam Raynor, I'm not sure there is anything you could say that would offend me. Being mistaken for my seventeen-year-old daughter isn't the worst thing that's ever happened to me." She turned and laid back down on her stomach.

"I'll just get to work here. So sorry," I said as I headed towards the shed. My face was burning hot and bright red, or so it felt. I was so embarrassed, I wanted to sprint home and lock myself in my room. I hoped Mrs. Autumn wouldn't tell Carolyn what I did, or that Carolyn wasn't around nearby and happened to see it. This was like walking into someone sitting on the toilet I thought, yet a bit sexier. I was sure this could destroy any chance I had with her. Hitting on a girl's mother was not the way to win a girl's heart. I searched the upstairs windows of their house but saw no sign of Carolyn. Maybe she wasn't home, I thought. I hoped.

I got the chainsaw and a shovel out of the shed and started working on the last stump. I couldn't help but look over at Mrs. Autumn constantly. I was seventeen years old, she was a MILF and totally topless. What's a guy supposed to do? I scanned the house windows periodically just to make sure Carolyn wasn't in there watching what I was doing. I was, however making progress on the stump, even with the sly MILF watching. After about an hour of digging and cutting with the saw,

I had the stump dug out deep enough to fill the hole with soil and spread some grass seed. The other stumps were cut out, but needed soil and seed as well. I put the tools away and grabbed some chlorine tabs out of the shed to put in the pool.

I turned the pool filter on and started skimming the leaves and bugs off the top of the water with a long handled net. I had a really good view of Mrs. Autumn from there. She was still lying out in the sun, now on her back. She had her eyes closed so I was free to gawk all I wanted, or so I thought. After about five minutes of staring and skimming I had worked myself up and had a full blown erection. The thin nylon workout pants combined with a penis that doesn't bend straight up makes for an interesting, if not disturbing sight. I was made aware of this when, after looking up at the upstairs windows for signs of Carolyn again, I looked back down at Mrs. Autumn and found her staring straight at my boner.

"You've had a hard day, haven't you, Adam?" Not knowing exactly the extent of what Mrs. Autumn was seeing I looked down. It was worse than I thought. It was so incredibly noticeable there was no way to play it off. I looked back at the pool not knowing what else to do or say. There was really nothing I could say.

"Jump in the pool, Adam, and cool off. It's a hot day," she said.

"Okay," I said. I didn't want to argue with her. She was a mother, I had fucked up twice already in a matter of hours, and I was not going to argue with her. Obviously she knew what I needed better than I did. I went to the diving board and dove right in. I stayed under the water as long as I could, not wanting to resurface and face her. Repeatedly I swam the length of the pool . I finally came up for air and leaned my arms on the tiles on the edge of the pool and floated there in the water with my back to Mrs. Autumn. After a few minutes I heard and felt the water from a splash. I squeezed my eyes shut, trying to calm myself down. After several seconds, which felt more like minutes, I felt a gentle tugging on the bottom of my shorts, like someone was trying to remove them, but not trying very hard. I turned around in a blind panic only to see Carolyn's face pop up out of the water with a grin.

"Hey slacker!" she said. She was happy, excited like a little kid on Christmas morning. Before I could respond she turned and was underwater again, gliding across the length of the pool. Before Carolyn could resurface I cast my eyes quickly over to where Mrs. Autumn had been lying, but she was gone.

CHAPTER TEN

Taking The Pot

I HAD CONFLICTED FEELINGS ABOUT WHAT had happened
that day. Part of me was totally freaked out. I had
intruded on Mrs. Autumn's topless sun tanning session
and called her sexy all in the space of a few seconds.
Then she had caught me all chubbed up while I was
staring at her, head in a daydream. I hadn't been able
erase the mental image of her breasts, at least not until
I took care of business, so to speak, and detailed the
entire experience in my journal. The other part of me was
almost exploding with excitement. The way Carolyn had
tugged at my shorts, the way she had said *hey stranger*, the
way she had hugged me before I left. The hour we had
spent in the pool together, racing and seeing who could
swim the farthest underwater, was incredible. She was
fun, light-hearted, and amazingly different from what
everyone at school had been allowed to see. She was

also quite athletic. I had initially planned to let her win some of the races, but found myself losing most of them, even though I was trying as hard as I could to beat her. I felt amazingly energized. I was also looking forward to hanging out with Mark and Joey again. I hadn't yet decided if I would spill to them all the details of what happened to me that day with Mrs. Autumn or not. I called Mark to see what he was up to for the night.

"Hey bud," I said, "what you doing tonight? Jerking it?"

"You scared, bitch? What you gonna do?" he said.

"Don't know. Wanna hang?"

"Yeah. Joey's over here. We'll cruise by your place."

"Cool, see ya soon," I said.

As customary, we found ourselves sitting on my back patio trying to figure out what to do. John was home with Stokes. Stokes had slept over the night before and was still at our house. It was seven at night and I would bet money he would be staying over again. Stokes was a hippie. He had long hair and stunk like patchouli oil. You could still smell him in the house twenty minutes after he left.

"What the hell is that smell?" my dad asked every time he left.

"It's patchouli oil, Dad. It's what hippies wear. It covers up their body odor." I would explain.

Again we had no access to booze with our only option leading to our last resort. My brother. We slunk down the basement stairs to John's door and knocked.

"Who is it?" he asked.

"It's me," I said.

"Go the fuck away, asshole," he yelled.

"Dude, it's Joey," Joey said, as if they actually liked him.

"Now you're definitely not coming in. Fuck off!"

"I got cash, dude. Let me in. I'll make it worth your while," Joey said. I heard someone rushing to the door. It was Stokes. He opened it up and a blast of patchouli hit me right in the nostrils.

"Fucking stinks in here," Mark said to Stokes.

"Blow me," Stokes said. "How much money you got?"

"I got enough to buy you guys a twelver if you buy us one," Joey said.

"Deal!" John yelled from his computer. "On one condition though."

"Fine, Mark, Adam, I won't blow you on the way to the store," Joey said.

"Nah, dude, that's not gonna do it this time," Stokes said.

"Who the fuck names their kid Stokes?" Mark asked, earning him a punch to his arm.

"Fuck man!" Mark yelled. "That hurt, dude!" I could

tell it hurt too. Mark's face was bright red. John got up from his chair and sauntered over to us. He clasped his hands behind his head and swung his elbows from left to right as he thought up some awful thing for us to do.

"Okay, creeps. I need you to go to the store and buy some stuff for me if you want us to buy you beer."

"Joey already said he would buy you beer," I said.

"I need some other shit too though."

"I don't have that much money, what do you need?" Joey asked.

"Here's the deal. You three go to the Grocery and pick up these items. One banana, one package of condoms, a jar of Vaseline, and…"

"And a bottle of hemorrhoid cream!" Stokes added.

"No fucking way, dude. I am not doing it," Mark said.

"Yeah, John, that's not even funny," I said

"You all have to walk up to make the purchase together. Stokes and I will be watching to make sure you do it. If you don't, no beer." A half hour later we were on our way to the grocery store.

"I don't like this at all, dude," I said to Mark as the three of us went into the store to buy the crap John had requested.

"I think it's hilarious!" Joey said. Joey thought my brother was some sort of god.

"Okay, here's what we'll do so we can get out of

there fast," I said, pulling out the list. "Mark, you get the bananas. Joey, you get the hemorrhoid cream and Vaseline, and I'll get the condoms."

"Why the fuck do I have to get the creepiest shit on the list? That's not right!" Joey said.

"We have to go up there together and buy all this shit. Who cares what items you get? Besides, hemorrhoid cream and Vaseline are both in the hygiene section, or whatever they call it"

"Fuck it. Fine. I'll get it," Joey said.

"Okay. Meet up front as soon as you get it. We'll check out quick," Mark said. I glanced at the check-out lines and saw the oldest lady in checkout three. She looked really nice and hopefully she wouldn't connect the dots. I was already embarrassed. John and Stokes stared at us from the front of the store. We each went our separate ways and met back up front with our items after a few short minutes. "Okay, let's fucking get this over with and let the old lady in line three check us out." I said. Looking around I saw that all the check-out lines were a little crowded. It was going to be impossible to be in the line alone.

"Okay, who's going to pay?" Mark asked.

"Joey is," I said.

"Why the fuck would I pay, dude? I just picked up a tube of hemorrhoid cream and Vaseline."

"Joey, you don't give a shit. You think this shit's funny. Mark and I don't," I said.

"Fuck it," Joey said. "Give me the stuff. I'll do it. I do know one thing though. You two are pussies, man." I gave Joey the money and he went and queued up. We followed him and stood behind him. Joey laid the items out on the conveyor belt. The fat lady in front of us finished purchasing her two frozen pizzas and we were greeted by a checkout woman wearing a name tag that read *Helen*.

"Good afternoon, boys," she said before she saw the items laid out before her.

"Hi Helen," Joey said way too loudly, a grin stretched across his goofy face.

Helen looked down and reached for the first item to scan. A banana--no big deal. Then she grabbed the Vaseline. Again, she swiped the jar across the scanner without blinking an eye. That's when she put her hand on the condoms. She paused, looked up at Joey, back down to the condoms, the hemorrhoid cream, and again at the bananas, and then looked up to me and Mark.

"Looks like you boys are having some kind of time tonight, huh?" she asked. I looked down, staring at my toes and Mark looked over at John and Stokes.

"You bet!" Joey said. I had been through Helen's checkout line before when shopping with my father. Dad was always friendly with her. He was in the store often enough to get to know many of the workers on a first name basis. I planned to avoid going to the store with my father in the immediate future lest we end up in Helen's line together.

We piled in the van together and sped toward the liquor store. The neon sign read Kareem's Spirits. John opened the door to run in.

"St. Paulie," Mark said as John's feet hit the blacktop.

"What?" John asked.

"St. Paulie. Grab us a twelve pack of St. Paulie."

"What's that?" Joey asked

"It's good beer. Not piss, like Budweiser and the rest of the domestic beers," Mark said.

"I agree. Let's drink good beer tonight. Let's celebrate," I said.

"Whatever," John said as he slammed the door and walked into the store.

"What are we celebrating?" Joey asked.

"Oh I don't know" I said "how about not having to ride the bus next year?" I didn't want to tell them I wanted to celebrate because I was giddy with excitement over Carolyn, our childhood friend who we had picked on growing up and who, at least to them, was a nerd.

"Fucking-A right," Mark said.

"Where we hanging tonight?" I asked

"Forest I guess," Mark replied.

"The Cobber is having a party tonight. He's home from U of I. There's going to be a shitload of people there. Rife with hotties. You guys should stop by, just don't tell John I keyed you in," Stokes said.

"TOGA, TOGA," Joey started chanting.

"What's that about?" Stokes asked.

"You know, a party, *Animal House*? The movie?" Joey said.

"I'm missing the connection bro. Anyway, just don't tell John I told you."

"Done," Mark said.

We dumped the twelve pack into the backpack and John dropped us off in the cul-de-sac away from Marks house. It was seven-fifteen in the evening and still hot out. Soupy, humid, smelling like freshly cut grass and dinners charring away on Webber grills. The Cobber's house was at least a mile from ours. He lived in an older part of town. His house was on more than an acre of land and had a huge fire pit in the backyard. I had been there many times growing up with John. They had been friends on and off since the first grade. We started our trek to the party.

"Why do they call Billy the Cobber anyway?" Joey asked.

"No shit," Mark said. "Why do they call him that?"

"Because when those guys were sophomores in high school, Stokes' mom was a nurse at Central Mercy Hospital. Stokes and John started a rumor that Stokes' mom was working in the E. R. and Billy, AKA the Cobber was transported in via ambulance to the hospital. Billy was allegedly rushed in on a stretcher; the sheets were covered in blood. They rushed him into radiology where they discovered he had something stuck up his ass," I laughed.

"A corn cob?" Mark guessed.

"Precisely, Watson." I said. "And it stuck. Everyone believed it at first, but then John and Stokes admitted that it was a lie. It had gone too far, even for them. They came clean, but the damage was done. Even though it wasn't true, everyone still calls him the Cobber. And to make matters worse, people started new rumors."

"Oh Man. That sucks. What other rumors did they start?" Joey asked.

"Someone else claimed they had a Polaroid of him jerking off in a bathroom stall in the men's locker room. He took shit for that one for several weeks, but the corn cob story was what stuck."

"Let's start a story about Mark!" Joey exclaimed.

"You fucking say anything about me and I will kick your ass so hard!" Mark said, then tried to punch Joey in the arm. Joey ran off and Mark chased after him. Mark was faster than Joey and after a brief chase caught him and threw him on the ground. Mark got his knees up on Joey's arms, pinning him down and started to wrench on Joey's nose.

"Promise you won't start any fucking rumors," Mark demanded.

"I promise dude, get off!" Joey yelled "You're getting my boogers all disturbed in my nose."

"You say any shit about me like that and I'll disturb more than your boogers. That's a god-damned promise," Mark said. I broke it up and we continued our walk to the home of the fabled Cobber.

There's a first for everything, and that night was our first real party, where excessive drinking was not only taking place but was expected. Alcohol induced make-out sessions and one-night stands were all within our grasp. We walked into the sprawling back yard and headed straight back towards the bon-fire pit and the cover of the forest. The night had finally sucked much of the heat out of the air and it now smelled more of cigarette smoke and pot than grass clippings. A CD player was set up on a stump near the fire pit and several longhaired guys were milling around it trying to orchestrate the night's musical score. It appeared they had consulted Stokes on proper evening attire as they were all dressed alike; Birkenstock sandals, ripped jeans and tie-dyed Grateful Dead shirts. Bob Marley was blaring at a volume a few decibels too high to be safe, and the portable player's speakers were pushing the sound out with really bad distortion. Thirty or so people were scattered throughout the yard and more were spilling out of the house onto the deck. A different crew ran the stereo on the deck and John was one of them.

"Let's crack these beers," I suggested. Joey opened up the backpack and distributed our beers. I twisted the cap but it didn't budge.

"Do either of you have an opener?" I asked. They didn't.

"So much for your fancy beer," Joey said.

"I'll get it," Mark said. He put a cigarette in his mouth, lit it for show, and walked up to the guys working the portable CD player. It appeared to go pretty well, because he stayed there chatting for the length of the cigarette. He slapped hands with the hippie's and returned.

"Very cool guys. Showed me how to open a beer bottle with a lighter."

"Seriously?" Joey asked.

"Yeah, I'll pop the next one and show you," He said as he handed us our beers. "They have weed too. They said they'd smoke us out if we wanted to party."

"Fuck that!" Joey said. We had made a pact long ago that whatever happened, we wouldn't do drugs. We would back each other up on that promise no matter what. This was the party where the lines would begin to blur. Everyone, it seemed, was smoking pot. It was beginning to be not as scary a proposition as it had been for us in the sixth grade.

"I don't know dude, it might be fun," Mark said.

"Dude, you'll do anything to fit in won't you?" Joey asked.

"Fuck off," Mark said as he pulled another Marlboro out of his pack and lit it.

We drank our beers next to the fire pit, listening to the music and trying to fit in. John had made it down to the fire pit by now and expressed his displeasure at us being present. We had to promise that we were never with him that night if we got busted for drinking when we got home. My parents wouldn't have freaked out if I got caught drinking a few beers, neither would Mark's. Joey's parents were a different story. He would be in deep shit. The official consumption count was Mark and I: eight, and Joey three, leaving only one beer left. Joey took this opportunity to try and get us to leave the party.

"Let's roll guys. I have to be home by ten-thirty," he said. He always had to be home by ten-thirty. Mark and I didn't have curfews really. If we were going to hang out late, we would just sleep over at one of our houses. Our parents didn't care. They were friends. We just had to call them and let them know.

"I'm not leaving yet, things are just getting going," Mark said.

"We're out of beer and I have to get home," Joey said.

"There are cases of beer growing out of the friggin' ground around here. We can get more beers," Mark said "Were going to stay longer dude." Joey looked at me.

"Yeah, bro. I am going to stay too. Sorry."

"Fuck. I'm just going to stay later too then," Joey said.

"You know you can't do that," I said. "If you're late your mom is going to be calling my parents and Marks ten minutes after you don't show. Then they'll all be worrying because your mom's freaking out."

"Man this sucks. You guys are assholes. We all came together. Nice way to blow me off," Joey said walking toward the street alone, dragging his feet as he began his walk home.

"Should we smoke some pot?" Mark asked with a big, stupid grin on his face.

"When in Rome," I said.

"Huh?"

"Never mind."

We found the three stoners who passed on the tribal knowledge of how to open a bottle with a lighter and approached them timidly. Mark asked if the offer to smoke with them was still open. It was, and they packed a bowl made out of nuts and bolts for us. They were already stoned and said it was all ours. Mark went first. He drew in long and deep while hovering the flame over the weed. The herb expanded as it burned and popped up and over the rim of the pipe. Mark was holding his breath when the involuntary coughing fit took over. I pushed the pot back down into the bowl and lit it up, imitating what Mark had done. The result was identical. The smoke travelled deep into the bowels of my lungs and set off a series of breath-stealing coughs that lasted several minutes. We then repeated the process several times. We finished the bowl and the coughing finally subsided, then uncontrollable laughter took its place.

Both of us forgot about drinking more beer and took turns trying to explain what we were thinking. I couldn't understand him, and he couldn't understand me. That was hysterical. Everything was funny. The muscles under my cheekbones ached from the perma-grin, and the ridiculousness of it all made me laugh even harder. I give Mark credit for having the mental faculty to realize we needed to get out of there, and fast. A few people had already begun laughing at us and in short order; we would have been the laughing stock of the party.

Our walk home seemed like something out of the

Twilight Zone. I would look down towards my feet and the sidewalk and get lost in thought. When I looked up and ahead of me, it felt like I was in another world. Mark and I didn't speak. We needlessly walked at a hurried pace. Upon arriving at my house, a short look shared between Mark and I communicated all that was needed to know. There was no way we could go into my house yet.

"Let's walk." I said.

"Yeah, where to?"

"Doesn't matter." We walked aimlessly for what seemed like an eternity until a new urgency came to bear. Hunger. The new prime concern. We arrived at my house to find my parents asleep upstairs in bed. We heated a frozen pizza and passed out on the floor in my room watching TV.

CHAPTER ELEVEN

The Morning after Hurt

I VAGUELY REMEMBER MARK GETTING UP to leave at some point. I got up to use the washroom and glanced at the clock radio: ten forty-five a.m. My head was pounding and the inside of my mouth felt scorched. As I urinated for what seemed like an eternity, I remembered that the night before I had smoked many more cigarettes than I was used to, not to mention the pot. *I smoked pot last night.* The thought cast an instant shroud of depression over me. Last night it was no big deal. I knew John and Stokes smoked pot, as well as most of their friends. But today, the morning after wandering around my neighborhood stoned out of my gourd, I had an overwhelming feeling of guilt weighing me down. The propaganda machine against drugs had been both a success and a failure. I spit in the eye of the caring administrators who had posted all the say-no-to-drugs posters on the school walls for as long as I could remember, as well as all the guest speakers that talked about the dangers of drugs before the entire student body in the gymnasium.

The successful part of those campaigns was apparent. They had succeeded in making me feel like I was a low life and a criminal. I had done something which I had been taught over and over again was horribly dangerous. I could only imagine what was to come next. I would be strung out on heroin and homeless, after-all, marijuana was a gateway drug, wasn't it? Doomed. I flushed the toilet and dragged myself back to my bed and lay down. I decided that I felt different. I started wondering if I was still stoned, then dismissed the thought as paranoia. I just needed more sleep. I thought of calling Mark to ask if he felt like I did but thought better of discussing it over the phone, again that damn paranoia. I wanted to be at Carolyn's but was in no shape to even get up, let alone work in the heat. I felt like shit. I thought about how the way I had felt the previous night just wasn't worth the price I was paying in the morning. I vowed I would never smoke pot again, but knew that it was only a promise I made to feel better about myself in that moment.

"Adam, you feeling okay?" my dad called from outside my bedroom door, startling me out of a deep sleep.

"Yeah dad I'm fine." I shouted back. I sat up and looked at the clock. One p.m. I got out of bed and opened my door. I wanted to get a reading on my dad. Had he known that something was odd last night? Or was that just my paranoia again? My dad was just reaching the bottom of the stairs with a full laundry basket in his arms. He turned and looked up at me.

"Sorry dad, I fell asleep reading." I said.

"No problem, I just figured you were up too late last night. I heard you guys come in and make something to eat. I hope you're not overdoing it. You know you should try and keep regular hours. Just because its summer doesn't mean you need to stay up so late and wear yourself down," he said. "You know you should have some quiet time every day as well. You've been on the go ever since you got out of school." Quiet time was an idea my father had thought up when John and I were young. One of the most annoying concepts my father had ever hatched. Since the second grade, during the summer I would have to spend one hour of quiet time in my room every day. I was to read or just be quiet alone in my room. It was nearly a forgotten relic of my childhood, but would make a re-appearance if I was tending to spend too much time with friends away from the house. Quiet time, I imagined was my father's way of bringing us back to home base. If John or I wanted to really annoy each other, we could suggest that the other had not been having much quiet time lately.

"I know. I just spent all morning in my room having quiet time dad."

"Alright. Just don't over-do it." My dad had a knack for knowing when something was out of place, or if I wasn't feeling quiet right. It was uncanny.

I went back into my room, closed the door and turned on the stereo. I shed my clothes and started running the shower. I noticed I had several nasty looking bruises and a few scrapes on my legs. I hadn't remembered doing anything the night before which would have caused them, but then again, I don't remember much of the night after smoking the pot. The water felt great as I imagined it washing away my crimes and self-perceived dishonor from the previous evening. I got out of the shower to hear Bob Dylan croaking out the song 'Knocking on Heavens door.' I became immersed in the words and considered if in my condition last night I was close to knocking on heaven's door. I brushed my teeth, picked out an outfit and got dressed for a visit to Carolyn's. My perspective on going to Carolyn's was changing. In my mind I was going to visit Carolyn first, and work in the yard was my second priority. I ran down the stairs two steps at a time to the kitchen. I opened a can of chicken noodle soup, microwaved it and began scarfing it down.

"Chew your food!" my dad warned. "You know that the whole digestive process starts with the chewing? You don't just swallow it whole. You should pulverize the food in your mouth before swallowing it."

"Right," I said, slowing down just enough to avoid his critical eye and another round of lecturing. I finished my soup without further incident, hugged my dad goodbye and walked to the Autumn's house for what would become another memorable evening.

CHAPTER TWELVE

Finally My Opportunity

I ARRIVED AT THE AUTUMN'S HOUSE at two p.m., much later than I had arrived before. I went straight to the back by the pool but no one was there. I was upset; I might have blown my chance to see Carolyn. I decided to mow the lawn, as this was the loudest thing I could do. Possibly she would hear the mower and want to come out to see me. I walked to the shed, started up the John Deer lawn tractor and backed it out. I drove the tractor up the yard towards the house looking for signs of life, hoping I hadn't missed some sign that Carolyn was home. I noticed my mow lines weren't straight and in spots missing small patches of grass between passes. I thought about my summer plans and how they had changed. On the last day of school I had imagined spending every day hanging out with Mark and Joey at the pool, making small talk with some girls at the volleyball courts. Now all I could think of was Carolyn Autumn, the nerdy neighbor girl. I was upset with myself for getting fucked up the night before, feeling like shit in the morning and not seeing Carolyn. I finished up the back yard and started on the front. A few passes in I saw Mark ambling toward me down the sidewalk like he owned it.

"Hey buddy," Mark said as he approached the tractor.

"Nothing runs like a John Deer," I said.

"So they say. What you up to tonight?"

"No plans. Felt like shit this morning, slept until one. How do you feel?"

"Tired. Just got up like twenty minutes ago. Parents fighting, so got the fuck out of there. Total bullshit."

"Sorry to hear that Mark. Anything I can do?"

"Nah. I'm gonna hit the gym, get my pump on. I'll call ya when I get home. You wanna hang?"

I didn't want to hang out. I had enough fun the night before and was still paying for it. I was hoping I could start hanging out with Carolyn at night.

"Not sure yet. Give me a call," I said.

"Don't be a pussy," he said, looking over at an approaching car.

It was Mrs. Autumn's red compact sports car. She pulled into the driveway and Carolyn was in the passenger seat. I looked back over at Mark. He was checking out the scene in the creepy way only Mark could do. They both got out of the car and Mark let out a wolf whistle. I was unsure who it was intended for, they both were dressed in short tennis skirts and tight white shirts. It was difficult to tell which one looked better. They both looked amazing. Carolyn waved and started to walk in our direction. I didn't want Carolyn anywhere near Mark and his wiener that was scabbed over from too much dry humping. I knew how he thought about girls and I didn't want him thinking about Carolyn like that.

"Hey guys," she said as she walked up.

"Hi Carolyn," I said.

"Looking good," Mark said as creepy as ever, making my blood boil. Mark gave me shit the other day for thinking she was cute and called her a ding bat. In our group, a ding bat was a funny term that had caught on and carried weight. It was a pretty bad assessment of someone. Carolyn gave Mark a funny look and then turned to me.

"You going to be around for a bit?" she asked.

"Yeah, I got some more stuff to do out back," I said, knowing I could find a reason to stick around.

"Cool. We just got back from playing tennis with my cousins. I wanted to talk to you about something. I'll be down in a bit," she said

"Okay," I said. She walked away toward the house without saying goodbye to Mark. I think she was offended

by the looking good comment, as well as the creepiness
exuding off him. He was glaring at her back.

"Not bad dude," Mark said. "You gonna hit that or
can I?"

"I like her Mark," I said. *What the fuck is with this kid?*
What made him think Carolyn would even consider him?
Like he could just have her if he wanted to. One thing
was for sure, the cat was out of the bag. Carolyn was no
longer the nerdy girl. I realized that soon every guy in the
school would be hitting on her.

"Settle bro, just messing around," Mark said.

"Yeah. Okay dude, I gotta get this shit done. Call me
later," I said.

"Sheesh, relax man."

"I'm fine," I lied.

I finished the last portion of the front yard and drove
around back to put the tractor away. The yard looked like
it had been cut by an amateur, which I was. The lines were
uneven and I had to re-mow where I had missed spots in
several places. I hoped Mrs. Autumn wouldn't be pissed.
I didn't want to fuck up a good thing. While closing the
shed I heard the back screen door bang shut. I looked
over and saw Carolyn standing on the patio, waving at
me. I waved back and walked over to her. She looked very
comfortable, wearing pink sweats and a white tank top,
and a seducing smile.

"You done for the day?" she asked.

"Yup, just finished."

Carolyn looked down at her bare feet and wiggled her toes, examining the nail polish I thought till she looked up at me.

"I'm making dinner tonight. I thought if you weren't doing anything, maybe you would like to join me?"

I smiled, if not beamed. "I would like that very much."

"Cool. My mom's going out tonight, so she won't be pestering us. Do you like pasta?"

"Love it."

"Great. I have a recipe I found in *Bon Appétite* that I wanted to make for a long time. You don't mind being my guinea pig?"

"Not at all, but it better be good, otherwise next time I mow the lawn I'm going to really botch it up. You know, miss spots and make it all uneven and shit," I said pointing to the yard.

"Oh very nice, I think you've found your calling." I looked at the lawn and shook my head.

"Six-thirty sound good?" she asked.

"Sounds good."

On my way home, once out of sight of Carolyn's house, I pumped my fist in the air and yelled, "fuck yeah." This was not something I would normally do. I was raised in a very reserved manner so expressing myself openly was out of the ordinary for me. My celebration over Carolyn asking me to dinner was taken directly from a page in Joey's book. Joey wore his emotions on his sleeve and I admired him for it. I had a recurring thought about how, if I were drowning, I would most likely not call out for help until it was too late. I was too embarrassed or shy to show I needed help, or to simply call out and make a scene. I remember growing up and going to parades with Joey and when the floats drove by they would throw candy at the crowd. I would stay back and pick up anything that landed right in front of me. Joey, however, would be running around half crazed, snatching candy from everywhere. I could learn something from Joey, except he was always over the top. I needed to find a middle ground.

I had a few hours to blow before dinner with Carolyn. The guilt and hangover from the previous night's pot adventure were gone and in its place was a sense of joy and enthusiasm. I considered buying her flowers, but felt that may be too presumptuous of me. She asked me to have dinner with her, that didn't necessarily mean it was a date did it? I decided against the flowers, but I felt I should bring something. After much thought, I decided on a bottle of wine. I figured I could try and match Carolyn's sophistication by bringing wine. The wine could also help lessen my anxiety that I was going to flub things up or act to nervous.

My dad kept a stash of wine bottles on the top shelf in his closet. They were special bottles he had bought or were given to him as gifts at holiday parties. Surprisingly my dad didn't mind if I had a glass of wine from time to time, or if I experimented with cigars or cigarettes, as long as it didn't become a habit. His father had been the same way when he was growing up. I considered asking my dad if I could have a bottle of wine from his stash, but then thought better of it. If he said no, I was shit out of luck. I wanted the wine so I nabbed a bottle, knowing he most likely wouldn't have counted them and, even if he had, he wouldn't really give a crap.

I showered while the stereo blasted a Bob Marley CD and I began to actually feel proud that I had smoked pot the night before. My intellect threw the bullshit-flag though and I resolved to not let Marley turn me into a pothead. Once in a blue moon, okay, but a regular thing was out of the question. I put on a clean pair of jeans and selected a red, short sleeved polo shirt from my drawer that my dad had dubbed 'the church drawer.' This drawer contained nicer clothes which I would usually only put on if I were going to church. I pumped a few sprays of my favorite cologne on my neck and one spray on my hand and rubbed it in. When I was a young child I noticed how when you shook hands with some men, if you smelled your hand you could smell cologne or aftershave. This intrigued me and I tried to emulate whatever these men had done to leave their mark.

I looked at the time on my clock radio and realized I had a half hour before I could leave for Carolyn's. I was so eager for the night to begin that I was ready with nowhere to go. I turned off the stereo, which was now annoying me, and lay on the bed. I ran scenarios through my head, trying to decide how I would act when I first saw her and what I would say throughout the evening. I was trying to figure out how to play it smooth and impress Carolyn, when someone knocked on my door.

"Come in," I said loudly and my father walked in.

"Looking good Adam, what's the occasion?" he asked, noticing I was all spruced up in church clothes and smelling like cologne.

"Carolyn Autumn invited me to dinner tonight. She claims she's a good cook," I said. He sat down on the bed beside me.

"That sounds like a wonderful time. She seems like a real class act. So doing some yard work over at the Autumn's house is starting to pay off huh?" My dad said, smiling and poking me in the ribs.

"Yeah, I'm excited. She seems really cool. We got to

talking more and more every day I have been there," I laughed.

"You guys will have a nice time. I know you don't need my advice, but I just wanted to share something that has always been helpful to me when going on a date with a lady. Just be yourself, that's all. If you're you and honest, and they like what they see, you have it made. If you try to be something you're not, you might win'em over for the time being, but when they find out who you really are, well, if they don't like it, you've lost out anyway. Give them the chance to like you right up front, 'cause Adam if they don't like a good guy like you, they don't deserve you anyway and you can do much better than that."

I smiled, "Thanks dad. That's good advice. I'll remember it."

My father gave the back of my neck a squeeze and walked out of the room, shutting the door behind him. I lay back on my bed and stared up at the ceiling. A wave of emotion rolled over me and my eyes began to tear over. Gratitude is the best way to describe the emotion which consumed me; gratitude for having such a great father and mother who were always there for me. I realized my plan to play Cool Hand Luke with Carolyn was ridiculous, and vowed to just be myself no matter how quirky that may be. If she liked me for me, I had it made.

After the half hour wait, that seemed more like hours,

I wrapped a sweatshirt over the bottle of contraband wine and headed out of the house. Before I hit the sidewalk I saw Mark and Joey walking toward me. *Fuck, not now. Why do they have to be here now? Look what I'm wearing.* Before I had time to concoct a story I wouldn't catch shit for, they were within shouting distance.

"What... The... Fuck...?" Mark said. Joey just laughed.

"Hey guys," I said

"You going to church or something?" Joey asked.

"Yeah Joe, I'm meeting your bible thumping cunt of a mom there. Don't give me any shit," I said, getting pissed off that I needed to explain myself. I could tell this was only the beginning of what would be a problem for our friendships, especially with Mark. He relied on me to be around to do things. Despite all of Mark;s machismo and posturing in front of Joey and I, he was too yellow to venture out of the house without us. He felt most comfortable if I was present.

"Chill out man, I was only kidding around, jeez," Joey said

"Where are you going anyway?" Mark asked.

"I'm going to Carolyn's," I said. It occurred to me that I could avoid catching shit if I acted like a dickhead and said I was going to go and get some pussy or something similar, but thought better of it. I liked Carolyn, and

Mark had already made annoying comments about her. If I ended up dating her, I didn't need Mark objectifying her further.

"Nice blow off move," Mark said.

"What do you mean blow off move. We didn't have plans," I laughed.

"Come on Adam, we always have plans. It's the fucking summer. Since when don't we hook up and hang out every day unless something un-fucking-canny is going on?" Mark said. He had me there. I hadn't let them know I wasn't going to hang out and it was sort of expected that we hung out every night.

"Sorry. I should have called and told you what was going on. Carolyn wanted to hang out tonight and I'm kind of into her," I said.

"Hey maybe if I asked Bridget out sometime we could double date," Joey said excitedly.

"Oh that's perfect," Mark said. "My two best friends ditching me for the home-schooled ding bat troll who no one ever sees in public, and the illegitimate love child of Mrs. Autumn, the biggest whore in the Midwest. Perfect. That leaves me where?"

"First of all, don't say shit like that about Carolyn. I know you don't like her mother, I get that, but the illegitimate ding bat part is just annoying dude. Carolyn never did anything to you but be nice. If a rumor like that got started it could really hurt her and that's not fair. You want me to start some shit about you whacking off like the Cobber?"

"I'm just pissed man. This better not be an every friggin' day thing," Mark warned.

"Okay," I said, more to end the volley than to agree. "I'll catch up with you guys tomorrow." Joey slyly made the 'call me' sign with his hand. Obviously about the double date with Bridget. We went our own ways that sunny afternoon, both literally and metaphorically.

CHAPTER THIRTEEN

Dinner Date

WHEN I RANG CAROLYN'S DOORBELL, she opened the door wearing a white dress that was contoured elegantly to her hips and seemed to float at her thighs. The thin spaghetti straps contrasted starkly to her pretty tan shoulders. She smiled, welcomed me and gave me a formal hug and kiss on the check. I was glad I wore my church clothes. She looked amazing; I felt unworthy.

"Come on in," she said as she turned and walked toward the kitchen. I took in her sweet perfume and watched her hair bounce lightly as she strode. I noticed that she was barefoot. *Now just don't stick your foot in your mouth. Remember, just be you.*

"This is a beautiful kitchen," I said admiring the dark granite countertop as she took foil off of something on the stove.

"Thanks. My mom loved to cook when I was little."

I unfolded the sweatshirt and pulled out the bottle of wine.

"I didn't know what to bring and didn't want to come empty handed so I brought this."

"Thanks Adam," she said taking the bottle. "I have some already chilled in the fridge. We can start with that." She placed a plate of stuffed mushrooms on the island and took out her bottle of wine, pouring us each a glass.

"I hate to have you waiting on me, can I help with anything?"

"Nope," she said in a higher tone "dinners in the oven, tables set. We're allll good." She sat down next to me.

"It's Riesling, I hope you like it. I like sweeter wine." I took a moment to taste it, hoping to get my own opinion of a wine I had never tried.

"It's nice, thank you."

"You got a late start today I noticed."

"Yeah, it's kind of a long, crazy story. One I would rather not share," I said, grinning.

"Well fuck that," she said. "No way am I letting you off that easy. Not with that kind of build-up. Nope, you're telling that story." She sat back crossed her legs and waited.

"You're serious aren't you?"

"Yup."

"I was afraid of that. Well, basically it's not that interesting, and you'll probably think I'm an ass, but here goes. We talked my brother into buying us some beer. We then went to a party some college dude was throwing and basically drank way too much. So I wasn't too perky this morning."

"That's it? That's your long story you didn't want to share?"

"Well yeah, that and I smoked pot and wondered around aimlessly for god knows how long before I could go back into my house." She almost spit her wine out as she choked back her laughter.

"Now that's more like it. That's a story." She paused, "Adam I'm different now. I'm not the annoying little girl you knew growing up. I just want you to..." I cut her off before she could finish.

"Oh I know. Trust me, I know," I said, raising my brow and shaking my head. She squinted and cocked her head sideways as if it may help explain my outburst. *Why did I have to say that? Now what? Explain she's a knockout and I was drooling all over the counter lusting after her? Just be honest with her like my dad said?*

"Well I just want you to know that I don't think of you like that. I mean, even though we haven't been hanging out together much, I like being with you is all."

"Thanks Adam. I like seeing you too. I know I have this reputation of being the goody two shoes and all."

"I don't think of you like that at all. I was worried you would think I was a loser because I smoked pot last night." I put a stuffed mushroom in my mouth and stopped talking. It was fantastic.

"What's wrong?" she asked.

"Mmph," I muttered as I began chewing again. "This is really good."

She perked up, sitting straight in her chair and reached out to take one herself. She put it in her mouth and chewed it slowly bouncing her head slightly from side to side.

"Too much parsley, but not bad," she said with a laugh. "Cooking has always been kind of a sanctuary for me. That and reading. I can get lost in a cookbook. I know it sounds weird, but I can read a recipe and it can spark lots of new ideas of things I could make. Reading books has always been an escape for me."

"I hear you on the books. I love to read as well. Now the cookbooks, that's a different story, but I sure am glad you like to cook. I can't wait for dinner." We finished our wine and she served up dinner in the dining room. It was amazing. Her cooking rivalled even my father's. Sweet potato ravioli in a jalapeño cream sauce and homemade pistachio ice cream for dessert.

Conversation during dinner came easily over a few more glasses of vino. We reminisced about days spent running around the neighborhood as little kids and I told her about my aspirations to become a writer. I knew Carolyn was smart, but I didn't know she was so well read. She had read most of the classics that I had, and was even more in key with the contemporary fiction lining the best seller shelves. Plus we shared a love of libraries. I was myself and held nothing back and she opened herself up like a book, allowing me to peer in. It was the most exciting night I may have had up to that point in my life. I was amazed that Carolyn Autumn was drinking wine and catching a warm buzz with me, not to mention the fact that she was stunning.

The wine was working as designed and was loosening my inhibitions to the point where I wanted to tell her how beautiful she was. The honesty was being tossed around pretty loosely and I was sure she was into me. This kind of back and forth flattery wasn't standard fare. Still, in my mind lingered the premise that Carolyn may just be different than anyone I had ever met. Possibly the warmth emanating from her was just the way she was, and not a thing more. Thankfully, it turned out not to be the latter.

Carolyn leaned back in her chair relaxed, holding her wine glass in front of her. I noticed the spaghetti strap of her dress had fallen off her shoulder and was hanging loosely at her bicep revealing the soft slope to her breast. At that moment I had an urge to protect her, cover her, and keep her safe, even from myself. I reached out and took the strap into my hand to place it back up on her shoulder. She anticipated my touch and reached up and stopped my progress with her hand and covered mine. Her head turned toward me and kissed my knuckles and lookup up into my eyes. I put my thumb to her bottom lip to feel its softness and she took the tip of my thumb to her mouth and kissed it. My previous experiences with girls had been scared, timid encounters.

When Carolyn put my thumb to her mouth and kissed it, all pre-planning, concerns and deliberation disappeared. What was left was pure desire, void of all the self-conscious bullshit I had previously experienced with Becky Hasting. I wanted to lean into her and kiss her, but felt unable without her permission.

"May I kiss you?" I asked.

She stood up slowly, still holding my thumb to her mouth and, with her other hand, pulled the front of her dress up slightly so that she could straddle my lap, and sat down on me. She leaned forward enclosing our faces by her sweet smelling hair and touched her forehead to mine. Her head turned sideways slightly and our lips met. The exploration was delicate, reminiscent of savoring some rare, sweet delicacy. I didn't think it was possible to get enough of her, to take enough of her in at that moment. No amount of her could be enough and I felt her trying to take in as much of me as she could as well. It was at this point that I noticed the tear that had rolled down her cheek and intruded on my taste buds with its saltiness.

"What's wrong?" I asked hoping she hadn't thought this was a mistake.

"I'm sorry Adam. It's just that it's been a hard year for me. I haven't really been able to share anything with anyone in a long time and tonight, being with you, well, I've forgotten about all that and I finally feel happy again."

"Is everything okay?"

"Everything is wonderful right now," she said, smiling at me and leaning in to kiss me again.

We lost track of time sitting there in the dining room kissing, and then sitting still just embracing each other. Conversation wasn't needed. We both just wanted to hold each other and take each other in. We were eventually interrupted by the door to the garage opening. We greeted her mom as she came in. She was dressed to kill the heart of any one-night stand and a bit tipsy. Carolyn quickly ushered me out the front door and told her mom we were going for a walk. We walked in the street toward my house as I slipped my hand into hers.

"Sorry about my mom," she said.

"Sorry about what?"

"You know the way she acts. She's obnoxious Adam, I know that. That's the main reason I have been so miserable lately. I know the reputation she has around town. I see the way people look at her when we're out in public and it's not good. It's a small town you know."

"I didn't realize. I'm sorry."

"Come now Adam, you didn't know my mom has turned into a floozy? Even kids at school that don't live near us make comments about her."

"I'm sorry Carolyn. Your mom's been good to me this summer, letting me work and all. I'm pretty grateful your mom had me over. Look at what she gave me," I said, holding up my hand which was still holding hers. Carolyn smiled at me and then reached up holding our hands up high.

"Thanks mom!" We both laughed hard at the goofy way she said it.

As we walked around the neighborhood I felt like I was hanging out with Mark or Joey. We were just being ourselves and joking around like old friends, but with the benefit of showing affection to each other. It was truly beautiful. I could have walked with her till morning, but it was getting cold and she was still only wearing her slight dress. I walked her home and kissed her good night at her front door.

"I want to take you somewhere tomorrow. If you want to go," she said.

"Are you kidding? Yes, I want to go."

"Can you use your parent's car?" she asked.

"Yeah."

"Awesome, what time should I be ready?"

"Eleven?"

"Perfect," she leaned in and kissed me again. "See you tomorrow."

Walking home I was full of excitement and replayed the events of the night over in my head. I wanted to tell someone about what a great time I had, but held back. I wrote down the details of the night as vividly as I could in my journal. Sleep came, but not after several hours of thought. It was as if my mind was an engine that wouldn't shut off. Every time I would try to clear my head and sleep, I saw Carolyn.

CHAPTER FOURTEEN

Twenty Questions

I WAS THE ONLY ONE OF my friends that spent my free time at the library. When I picked Carolyn up and she directed me to take her to the library, I was elated. The town library had recently been renovated. It was an "architectural experiment gone horribly wrong" my father had said. The ceiling was unfinished, revealing all the inner workings of the beast. The air conditioning and heating ducts, electric wiring, phone and Internet cabling were all in plain sight, giving the feeling, at least to me, that I was inside a massive computer mainframe. The roof was made from copper roofing shingles, which was apparently a big deal to the city. A newsletter was sent to all the town residents prior to completion of the library, boasting the modern energy-saving and efficiency innovations used.

If you were at the library when it was raining, you

could hear the constant battery of rain drops. During a heavy down pour it was startling how loud it got, giving the impression the weather was much worse than it really was. Regardless, I enjoyed going to the library on a rainy day. I was good at judging what the weather was *really* like just from the sound on the roof. Carolyn said she could only use the library as a place to read *half* the time. That was because she devoted half her time to reading classic literature, the other half, contemporary. Reading anything pre-1970 in that library "doesn't feel right" she mentioned.

Carolyn used her library card to check out one of the newly added meeting rooms. You could use the rooms for three hours at a time. If no one else needed it, you could use it all day.

I wanted to spend all my time with Carolyn. I know that would hurt Mark and Joey as it was breaking up the routine we had going on for so many years. We had seen it happen before. Boy and girl meet and they both ignore their friends completely for one another.

We settled into our private room at the library and sat at an empty table. We had nothing to read.

"Now what?" I asked. I was feeling a bit uncomfortable of the unknown.

"Whatever you want."

"Okay then, what's your favorite color?"

She smiled. "As good a place to start as any I suppose. Red, if it's for a dress or lipstick, pink for nails or a bra. Let's see, oh, green if we're talking about crayons, black for boots and nylons, unless were talking about cowboy boots. White for teeth and watch bands, brown for purses and eyes, unless the dress is formal, or the eyes are yours of course, because yours are hazel. How about you?"

"Wow," I said. "You've really set the bar high haven't you?"

She smiled. "Come over here. Come closer."

I did what she said and she kissed me. I thought how Carolyn had transformed herself in such a short period of time, from a shy timid girl into a confident young woman who knew what she wanted and reached out to obtain it.

We wanted to know everything about each other. We played a game for hours where we would write quizzes for each other, twenty questions each. It could be anything from our favorite color to our most embarrassing moment. Hundreds and hundreds of questions between us and we started to get to know each other very well. We shared with each other our dreams, like the authors whose books filled the shelves in the library. Exposing myself to someone else was scary, but I trusted Carolyn, and she trusted me. We shared our fears and secrets. She didn't judge me, nor I her. The solid foundation of our relationship was formed in the meeting room that day.

Carolyn had invited me over for dinner again that Friday night. We assumed her Mom would be going out as she usually did. We were wrong. The plan was to order pizza and watch a movie, but when the pizza arrived and Mrs. Autumn was still there, Carolyn and I invited her to join us.

"I don't want to bug you guys," she said. "I'll keep out of your hair."

"It's okay Mom, really. Have some pizza," Carolyn said.

"Well, if you share your pizza I'll share my wine."

Carolyn and I smiled at each other. This was turning out better than expected. We drank wine and ate pizza with Carolyn's Mom. After that, Carolyn took out a deck of cards. She taught her mom and I how to play a game called speed. It was a frantic fast paced game that brought out the competitiveness in each of us. We were loud and unrestrained from the wine. It was like a dream spending the night with these two beautiful women.

We spent more and more time at Carolyn's house. Out by the pool during the day, and inside hanging out in the kitchen at night. Mrs. Autumn was still out on the town over the weekends, but was around more and more during the week nights. Carolyn's opinion of her mother and her relationship with her had improved drastically since we started spending more time around the house with her. I could tell Mrs. Autumn was becoming a different woman. It was because she was enjoying spending time with us, and she was actually fun to be around. I had begun to consider my girlfriend's mother a friend of mine. It was an odd feeling. On a few nights, we all got pretty drunk together.

One night in particular she opened up to me more than usual. We were also more drunk than normal. We were sitting on the back patio near the pool listening to music and smoking cigarettes. Carolyn had gone in to the bathroom.

"Sometimes I think about leaving this neighborhood," Mrs. Autumn confided.

"Why's that?" I asked.

"Things are just different here now. I used to be friends with everyone in the sub-division. Now, some people won't talk to me. I get fucked up looks. Asshole husbands blame me for their wives running off and stuff. I have nothing to do with that. I can't believe I'm even talking about this with you."

I looked at her and saw she was starting to tear up. I looked down and noticed her feet, they were so god-damn sexy. I didn't want to get into this conversation with Mrs. Autumn. I didn't want to explain that Mark thought the way she just described. The alcohol provided me a quick wave of confidence and the solution. I flicked my smoke in the yard and grabbed her by the shoulders and shook her. It was an opportunity to touch her.

"Snap out of it. You need healing!" I put my palm on her forehead and pushed her head back. "You're healed!" I shouted. She lost her balance a bit from the push and the wine. I did it again. This time she almost fell over and was laughing so hard that she couldn't quite catch her breath.

"You fucker," she managed to say.

Carolyn came out and looked at us like we were crazy. "What did I miss?"

"Oh, not much, just a quick exorcism," I told her.

"Let me show you," Mrs. Autumn said, and tried to do it to Carolyn. Carolyn fought back and they ended up losing their balance and falling down on the patio. They both laid on their backs, looking up and laughing, then catching their breath. I laid down too and we stayed there a good long while, listening to music and looking up at the stars.

CHAPTER FIFTEEN

Millinocket, Maine

MY PARENTS HAD PLANNED FOR us to spend the Fourth of July week in Millinocket. I loved going to the cabin during that time because the town did their fireworks display over the lake. My brother and I would take the pontoon boat out on the lake, lay across the open astro-turf bow and watch the display. The view from the boat was surreal. The colorful mushrooming of fireworks high above filled the sky with brilliant color. The biggest and brightest ones would illuminate the tree lined banks of the shore and reflect on the water. In spite of all that, neither John nor I wanted to go this year. John because he wanted to party with friends, and myself because it meant leaving Carolyn. The last two weeks consisted of nothing but Carolyn and that was the way I wanted it. My parents demanded we both go, but relented somewhat and allowed John to stay with Stokes. I, however, had to go. I threw a fit and told my parents I wanted to spend the Fourth with Carolyn. My Dad figured it out quicker than I did.

"Let's take her with then," he said. "Since John isn't going we have an empty room at the cabin." This was the best of both worlds. I could go to the cabin, which I loved, and share the experience with Carolyn. I just had to get her parents to approve. This approval was easier to obtain than I anticipated.

"You've given my Mom a gift," Carolyn explained. "Now she can do whatever it is she does without me in the way all week."

The drive to Millinocket was always a nightmare. Twenty two hours in the car with my parents and John. The drive this year, however, was over in a flash. Carolyn and I planned what we would do during the drive. We bought a nice leather bound journal and wrote most of the trip up to Maine. We agreed we would take turns writing the story. We didn't determine the length of the story; it could be a short story, a novella or an epic tome of a novel. The only stipulation was that we could write no more than two pages in the journal before we had to hand it over for the others turn. We both took painstaking care to develop the story and make the details of the pages as vivid as possible. Carolyn proved to be a worthy traveling companion. She didn't fart, nor did she stretch out and hog most of the back seat with smelly feet. We drove straight through. My Dad took the first shift, my Mom the second, and I took the last leg. We arrived in Millinocket with a journal that was over half written in.

The first order of business upon arriving at the cabin was always the same for John and I. First of course, we would get out of the car stretch, taking in a deep breath of the fresh Maine air. The ever-greens provided a year round reminder of Christmas. Even before going into the cabin and bringing our bags in, we walked the sandy path to the lake. It was different each year. It may smell like dead fish, have loads of sea weed at the shore, or the water level may be higher or lower than how we left it. This year it looked perfect. Of course the final test would be how warm the water was.

"It's awesome here, Adam," Carolyn said. I looked at her to make sure she wasn't just being polite. I could tell she meant it.

"Could you imagine living here year round? Waking up and walking down here every morning before school or work. Listening to the sound of the birds, watching squirrels and deer out your window. Why wouldn't everyone want to live like that? Why does anyone want to live in a city?" I asked.

"Where do you buy designer shoes or purses from around here? Where is the nearest Victoria's Secret? Some people think they can't live without that kind of stuff. I could trade it all in to live here," she said.

"Sure, Mrs. fancy underpants," I said. "I can see you wearing some big old bloomer drawers from the hardware store," which was the main source of everything in Millinocket Maine. Even underpants.

"Is that what you think I'm wearing?" she said coming up to me and kissing me softly on the lips. Carolyn and I had spent plenty of time hugging, kissing and cuddling during movies (not *Die Hard* though), but we hadn't done anything more than that. I respected her so much that I didn't want to suggest something she wasn't comfortable with and blow it, so to speak. I also didn't want to miss an opportunity to act when she was giving me the OK, or hinting that it was okay to move forward with her. Lately, I was getting the impression from her that she *wanted* me to move forward, be more sexually active. In our common parlance, go to second or third base or maybe even *do it*. This was one of those times I sensed she was urging me on. Like a game of tennis, volleying the ball onto my side of the court, and then she would wait. I took the opportunity to volley back.

"No, I don't think that's what you're wearing. But I bet they are soft," I said sliding my hand down her back. I lifted up the back of her shirt and slipped my fingers down the back of her sweat pants. What I felt was intoxicating. The soft, luxuriant silk on her muscular toned, but still soft ass drove me to kiss her passionately. She reciprocated, reaching down to my thigh and gliding her hand up my leg to my groin. She felt for the first time, with what I imagined was horror, my deformed penis, bending down instead of up. She didn't pull her hand back in shock, nor did she linger too long. What she had done was confirm that she had been providing subtle cues that she wanted, and would allow, more.

"You're amazing," I told her.

"I'm glad you think so," she said as she leaned into me and bit my ear hard before running off laughing towards the cabin.

I introduced Carolyn to all the ritualistic things John and I did when we were there. Night hikes without a flashlight, bon fires on the shore, skipping rocks on the lake, and snorkeling for craw fish. Carolyn wouldn't grab them, but she would lift the rocks for me while we searched for the biggest ones. Although I had done all these things for as long as I could remember, doing them with Carolyn was like them for the first time.

The day of the Fourth of July we all went to town to stock up on groceries for our last three days. While my parents were shopping and Carolyn was looking at the magazine section, I stole away to the pharmaceutical counter and laid the three-pack of condoms I had selected on the counter. I checked out as fast as possible and pocketed the rubbers. I was paranoid that Carolyn would see or feel the bulge in my pocket. I didn't want to be presumptuous.

Dinner consisted of steak, garlic shrimp and corn on the grill. My parents were drinking wine and allowed us both to have a glass. Carolyn assured my parents that hers would not mind if she had some and said it was very European of them to allow her to. My parents found this hilarious and we all had a good time over dinner on the back deck. The sun began to sink and my parents had continued to enjoy the wine. I told my parents Carolyn and I wanted to watch the fireworks from the pontoon boat. They agreed to let us go, but not until we were provided with a dissertation on the dangers of being out on the water.

"Even a small lake can be treacherous Adam. If the engine quits, you could be done for," dad explained. "Even if you had an oar you would basically be chasing your tail, going around in circles!"

I laughed, and Carolyn and my Mom laughed along with me. My Dad feigned hurt feelings for not being taken seriously and walked off, only to return shortly with two life jackets, a set of oars and a flair he kept in the trunk of his car. He demanded we take them with us on the boat in case we got into a *tight spot*. I got two blankets, a pack of Marlboros, and the rubbers from the cabin and we pushed off shore shortly before sun down. I motored us out onto the glass smooth lake to a secluded bay with no houses in sight. We took our blankets and laid them out on the artificial turf flooring of the boat and settled in. The sound of crickets and frogs reverberated from the shoreline. Out over the lake, where the horizon met the water, burned the last remnants of pink and orange.

"It's beautiful isn't it?" I asked her. Both of us leaning back on our elbows.

"You know what it is?"

"What?"

"The suns farewell. A gift to us after a perfect day together, and the beginning of a perfect night." Carolyn climbed assertively on top of me and pulled my shirt off before removing her own, as well as her bra. We kissed for a few minutes and then she hurriedly repeated the process by removing our pants.

We made love for the first time on July Fourth, under the fireworks. At first our hearts raced with panicked sexual tension but then gave way to perfect contentment and open exploration. After that evening, every spare minute we found ourselves alone together was spent fucking like rabbits.

CHAPTER SIXTEEN

The Consequence of Summer Love

I MANAGED TO GET THROUGH THE rest of the summer without catching much shit from Mark and Joey, even though I had blown them off completely. I spoke to Joey once or twice and learned he was now dating Bridget, the home schooled girl. That left Mark to fend for himself. The week before school started back I gave Mark and Joey a call but was only able to get through to Joey. Things had not been going well with Mark he explained.

"He's fucked up man. Been hanging out with a bunch of hippies and shit. I think he's doing a bunch of bad shit. I told you fuckers..." I cut him off.

"Hold on Joe, what's he doing?" I asked

"I don't know dude. I haven't hung out with him in a month. He doesn't return calls, if I stop by he will answer the door, but he won't invite me in. He's not the same. You fuckers smoked pot and now I bet he is trying everything."

"Chill out Joe, I'm sure he's not trying *everything*," I said. "I'll stop by and see him this afternoon. I'm sure he's just pissed at both of us for blowing him off this summer."

I went to Marks house that afternoon. I felt guilty because I didn't really want to see him. I assumed I would catch shit from him for not hanging out. I was prepared to apologize and try to get him to see things from my perspective. I didn't have to explain, and the conversation didn't lend itself to an apology. If anyone had any explaining to do it was Mark. As soon as he opened the door it was as if I was looking at a different person. His face looked gaunt and emotionless and he had lost weight. His already limited vocabulary had changed too. Lots of *right ons,* and *far outs* thrown into the mix. So many in fact that I called him out on it.

"What the fuck is far out?" I asked. "You sound like you've been surfing all summer or something."

"Whoa dude, don't get heavy on me. I'm not into that right now," he said. "Just be cool man." Mark was jittery and tweaked out of his gourd. I didn't know what he was on, but I knew it wasn't pot. I had seen plenty of stoned dumb asses and this was different.

"What are you on?" I asked.

Mark laughed in a high, irritating pitch, like a hyena. "I'm high on life dude, don't you know?" he said.

"Where are your folks?"

"They're as good as divorced. My Mom moved out a few weeks ago," Mark said, beginning to laugh maniacally again.

"I'm sorry, Mark."

"Don't worry bro, Mrs. Autumn is probably taking good care of my mom. She caused all this. She fucked up my mom just like her daughter is fucking you up."

"I don't see it that way Mark. At least, not all of it. Mrs. Autumn may have got a bunch of these hens stirred up, including your mom, but leave Carolyn out of it. I don't want it weird between you and her."

"Fuck that. I can't stand that family and you're killing my buzz," Mark said before turning, and closing the door in my face. I banged on the door and called his name.

"Fuck off," he yelled.

I went to Carolyn's. I was upset and wanted to talk to her about what happened. Carolyn and her mom were laying out back by the pool. Mrs. Autumn was smiling at me as she sat up.

"Now I know you two love birds have really hit it off this summer, but don't you go knocking her up," she said.

"Mom!" Carolyn cried, covering her face with her hands.

"Well, I'm just saying, you guys need to be careful. If you need any condoms you just let me know. Okay?" I stood there unable to form a response. "It's okay, Adam. I know you and Carolyn are sexually active. I'm not upset. I just want you to be safe. Promise me you will wear protection," she demanded. I promised I would. Carolyn jumped up, grabbed my hand and pulled me into the air conditioned house. We went up to her room and sat on the bed.

"You told your mom?" I asked. "What the fuck?"

"It's okay Adam, she doesn't care. Girls share that kind of stuff with their moms. I didn't know she would say something to you though. I'm sorry."

"Oh boy," I said. "Listen, I'm worried about Mark. I think he's fucked up on drugs."

"What?" Carolyn asked. "Why do you say that?"

"Joey told me. I just stopped by his house and he's whacked out. Something's not right with him."

"Let's go over there," she offered.

"No, he won't talk to me. We just got into an argument and he told me to fuck off."

I explained everything. How Mark blamed Mrs. Autumn for getting the woman in the neighborhood worked up, how his parents were divorcing and that he was jealous of Carolyn. She took it all pretty well considering. She was quiet while I explained the situation. She didn't dispute her Mom's bad influence on the woman in the neighborhood, although I could see she was hurt by it.

"You need to be there for him Adam. If he needs help, you need to try," she said.

I agreed, but didn't know how to help someone who didn't want to be helped.

"I know what you need," she said, leaning down to her nightstand and pulling out a brown bag containing at least a hundred condoms.

"What the hell is that?" I asked.

"They're condoms."

"I know, but where did you get all those?" I asked, afraid I already knew the answer.

"My mom." I shook my head while Carolyn unwrapped and began putting on me the first of many condoms supplied by Mrs. Autumn. Carolyn once again distracted me from thinking about anything but her.

That night I wrote the following in my journal:

> *Life is full of ups and downs. The low points help*
> *accentuate the highs. I have gone a good long while*
> *without a low and am becoming concerned. I feel I*
> *have been living in a fairy tale and pray I am let*
> *down gently when it all comes to an end.*

CHAPTER SEVENTEEN

The Ending to My Fairy Tale

OUR SENIOR YEAR BEGAN. So did worrying about the future. It was my new hobby. I was worried about what would happen to Carolyn and I if we both didn't get accepted to University of Iowa, where we decided to try and go together. I was worried about Mark; I only spoke to him occasionally in passing at school, when he decided to show up. He looked like hell. I had tried to have a heart-to-heart with him a few times, but that just pushed him further away.

"I'm worried about you," I said. "People are talking, saying you're a junky and shit."

"Fuck them. Since when do you care what people think?"

"You used to care. You used to care a lot. How about the Cobber? You sure cared when Joey threatened to start a rumor about you like the Cobber."

"Apples and oranges. Some assholes saying I am doing drugs is a lot different than my best friend telling the student body I stuck corn in my asshole," he said.

"Not really," I argued

"Fuck off, Adam, Okay? Can you do that for me? I don't need your shit," he said as he huffed off. The rumor was he was taking heroin. It was now fashionable to snort it. Shooting it was for junkies, but snorting was different and didn't cross that imaginary line. No tracks, no dirty needles to share and no trips to pharmacies to purchase them.

I talked to my dad about Mark. I told him I thought he was taking drugs. My dad, of course, reacted instantly and wanted to call his parents straightaway. My instinct was to protect Mark from that. I circled back and assured my dad I didn't have enough information. I told him it could just be a rumor, the rumor being that he may have smoked pot. This was enough to reign my father back in.

"Well gosh darn Adam, I can't go calling his parents and telling them someone started a rumor about him," he explained. I was confused. I didn't know the right thing to do. Ratting Mark out would be the ultimate betrayal. I knew exactly how he would respond; he would never speak to me again.

Mark, Carolyn and I all got used cars for our senior year. Carolyn and I drove together every morning and took Joey. His parents couldn't afford another car, but Joey didn't care. Carolyn and I would double date with him and Bridget on weekends. Joey and Bridget had become pretty serious. They spent as much time together as Carolyn and I did. Carolyn and I found it funny how god-damned old fashioned and respectful Joey always acted towards Bridget. He had her trained to actually sit in the back seat until he got out and opened the door for her. Chivalry was not dead to Joey.

Carolyn was excited about the prom. I was indifferent. Joey was going with Bridget, and Mark actually got in the mix and was going to go with us. He was going with a girl I had not met. She was from the high school on the other side of town. To me the best part of the prom would be that our circle of friends would be back together again. The goal was no longer to get laid, been there, done that. Maybe this would turn things around for Mark. I imagined Mark, Joey and I could start going on triple dates. I hoped Mark would become more interested in his girl like I had Carolyn and then he would have less time for drugs. Wishful thinking.

Prom preparations were handled by Carolyn. She was the most organized and volunteered to get everything in order. The plan was to take a limo to dinner at a nice place prior to prom, then hit the prom for about an hour and a half, then skip out and head to a cheap hotel nearby and get drunk. The hotel was called Passerby's. It was cheap but you didn't get hassled there for being under twenty-one and bringing beer into the rooms. That was the least of their worries. Of bigger concern to the local authorities was that there were hourly room rates. Carolyn thankfully planned it so that we all had our own rooms. They were all in a row and had interconnecting doors.

The night of prom we all met at my house so that my father could take photos. Carolyn and Bridget both looked stunning. They wore beautiful, sequined dresses and had their hair done and nails painted together. We all presented ourselves formally to match the occasion, greeting each other with a hug and kiss to the cheek. Like the game kids play where you pick the items that are out of place, there was Marks date, Bethany. She wore a long colorful hippy dress that looked to be left over and preserved from the late sixties or early seventies. She had ginormous boobs and they were spilling out of her dress. She hadn't worn a bra or shaved her pits for the occasion. She smelled like hippy oil, wore sandals and carried a leather purse.

"Do you see those tits?" Mark said while my father was taking a group photo of the girls.

"Indeed," I told Mark. "It's hard not to.."

"I'm going to fuck those tonight dude. You might even see them. We're all going to be in the same block of rooms. We'll have these chicks buck naked in no time," he said. I glared at him.

"Mark, I'm not in for that. I'm sure Carolyn isn't either. Fuck, I can guarantee Mrs. home school over there is not into it either."

"God-damned buzz kill. You know, you've really changed," he said. I shook my head.

"Let's just try and enjoy the night dude. You look like you have plenty on your hands with Bethany. She should keep you entertained." Mark got excited again for the night and wore his disgusting face as he stared at Bethany.

We took our limo to the nicest restaurant in the area, a steak house. Dinner was fantastic. Fantastic to everyone but Bethany, that is. Of course the girl wearing the leather purse and sandals is the only vegan in the group. Not only was steak out of the question, but everything on the menu except a house salad. The pasta sauces all contained cream, and milk was for baby cows. The only thing she had to eat was that salad prior to a night of drinking.

The prom itself was boring as expected. We visited with some of our friends around the ballroom, Joey and I enjoyed some slow dances with our dates and Mark groped Bethany during several songs on the dance floor. He was starting to act even more strange than usual; I just knew he was on something. He had to have taken something between dinner and the prom. He was jittery now and seemed ready to jump out of his skin. Bethany, on the other hand, looked like she was about to fall asleep; like she'd taken something too. The girls were talking to a few friends when Joey pulled me aside.

"Notice anything unusual about Mark and Bethany?" he asked.

"Yeah, they're high as kites. We should get him out of here before the Dean notices." I said.

"Yeah, not a bad plan. He's totally hyped up. Do you think he's doing coke?"

"No clue," I said, "but what's really bothering me is Bethany. Don't you find it odd that Mark is bouncing off the walls and she seems to be about to pass out?"

Joey stared at me in surprise. "I'm not saying Mark would give her ruffies or anything but shit."

"This isn't good" Joey said.

"Let's not get all worked up yet. Let's just get out of here, quickly."

Joey rounded up the girls and I went out onto the dance floor to get Mark and Bethany.

"Bro, we got to go," I said. He just laughed.

"We just got here dude, check this out." He dipped Bethany low and came up grinning. I looked around the room and noticed several faculty members eyeing us and talking behind their hands. Panic began to set in.

"Mark, we need to get out of here now. Faculty are staring at you and you look like you're all fucked up." This time Bethany laughed. "I'm leaving you both here if you don't follow me out right now." I said, and I turned and strode off to gather our party so we could leave. Just before I reached them, the Dean caught me by the arm and asked if we were having fun. I knew he was trying to ascertain if we were all on drugs or not. He was standing closer than was comfortable, like he was trying to smell if I had alcohol on my breath. I exchanged niceties with him only long enough to demonstrate I was, in fact, sober. From the corner of my eye I saw Carolyn at the exit pushing Mark and Bethany out the door, and Joey and Bridget bringing up the rear.

I checked our group in at Passerby's and paid the man at the counter. He reached out the keys towards me but hesitated.

"I don't want any trouble now; do you hear me?" the man asked. He looked between me and Mark behind us.

"Yes sir, you won't hear a peep from us." He seemed to be convinced by my words and handed over the keys. Mark had the furthest room, followed by mine, then

Joey's. We brought our bags in and unloaded the booze we each brought onto Marks bed. Carolyn and I each had a bottle of red wine we'd lifted off our parents. Joey had a bottle of Kahlua.

"What the fuck is that?" Mark asked, wrinkling his nose.

"It's Kahlua," Joey said.

"Yeah, no shit asshole. Who drinks Kahlua?"

"I love Kahlua!" Bethany said in a sulky voice.

"It's all I could get," Joey said. "My parents don't drink okay? Someone gave this to my parents for Christmas years ago." Bethany cracked open the seal and took a big chug straight from the bottle. Mark had a bottle of Vodka and a large bottle of cranberry juice. We drank for about an hour and were having a pretty good time, until Mark pulled out a bag of weed.

"What the fuck is that?" Joey asked.

"It's weed, dude." Mark said and stared at Joey incredulously.

"I don't want to be anywhere near that shit dude," Joey said.

"Your loss," Mark said as he packed a bowl. Joey retreated to his room with Bridget and closed his door.

"Why do you have to be that way?" I asked Mark

"Man is he uptight," Bethany said.

"What dude, Beth's right. Joey's going to college next year. You think people in college don't smoke weed?"

"I want to try it," Carolyn said quietly.

"Yeah, but dude, you know he's uncomfortable. Now he's going to hole up in his room all night," I told him.

"Yeah right" he said "he's probably going in there to fuck her brains out!" I shook my head and relented.

"Let's get stoned," I said.

We were bouncing off the walls. Carolyn and I took turns babbling on and on, while Mark and Bethany laughed at our inexperience. They were just as fucked up, but just used to being so. We were having a great time. Bethany kept occasionally chugging down the Kahlua. Carolyn and I were drinking water in an attempt to remedy seemingly incurable cases of cotton mouth. We lost track of time, but after a good long while a slow song came on the radio.

Mark started kissing Bethany on the bed. This was my cue to get the hell out of Dodge, and Carolyn and I retreated to our room. We closed the connecting door most of the way. We knocked on Joey's door and he opened it a crack.

"You okay?" I asked. He was smiling. I could tell he was enjoying himself with Bridget. I wasn't sure what that entailed but at least he was having fun. Carolyn and I took a long shower together prior to jumping into bed. We fucked, more so because doing it on prom night was expected, rather than because we were horny. We were tired from smoking pot and drinking wine. I mostly wanted to get in bed and cuddle while watching a movie on the free HBO; *Die Hard* was on.

We were startled awake by the most repulsive sound I have yet to encounter. It was Mark grunting while fucking. Along with the sound he was making was the sound of the head board banging against our shared wall. I was sure this was to some degree for Joey's and my benefit. It was just like Mark to try and be as loud as possible, to try and *impress* us. Carolyn cuddled into me.

"This is kind of scary," she confided.

"Yeah. I'm sorry. I would never have come here if I knew you would have to hear that," I said. The grunting from Mark became violent. Joey knocked on our door and I called for him to come in.

"Dude, what the fuck is that?" he asked.

"It's Mark, I guess."

"Is she okay in there?" he asked. "That doesn't sound normal."

"It doesn't Adam," Carolyn said, "and I don't hear her." We were all freaked out; no gentleman would make sounds like that. We were all afraid of the kind of person who would make those sounds. Even though we knew Mark well, this was not right. Once the phone started ringing in their room I decided I had to find out if Bethany was okay before the man at the front office started knocking on the door.

"I'll take a look," I said, standing up. I walked over to the unlocked door and slowly turned the knob. I pushed the door open just enough to fit my head and peered in. The smell of Kahlua and vomit smacked me in the face and instantly turned my stomach. Mark was laying on his back on the bed, Bethany kneeling on top of him in reverse cowgirl position. Mark was humping up into her hard, still grunting. She had been sick from the bouncing and vomit was covering her tits, stomach and thighs. Leaves of salad, like children's stickers, were covering her body. She looked like a zombie, mascara running down her face. She was half awake but staring directly at me, expressionless.

Whatever after party took place when we left them earlier in the night must have been pretty intense. Neither of them had the faculties to realize they were fucking in vomit. I turned into our room and made it to the bathroom just in time to hurl in the toilet. Carolyn must have looked in because she ran in and started puking in the tub. Joey and Bridget were soon gagging as well. After emptying our stomachs, we tried to compose ourselves.

"This is worse than I thought" Joey said "we need to help him Adam. He's going to end up dead if he keeps this shit up."

"Joey's right. You guys need to do something." Carolyn said.

"What, tell on him? Narc him out?" I asked

"Exactly." Carolyn said. Joey agreed.

"You know he may never talk to us again." I said.

"You won't be able to talk to him if he's dead either." Carolyn reasoned.

Bridget was crying. "No wonder my parents home schooled me!" she shouted. "I want to go home."

Carolyn took her by the hand and brought her back into Joey's room. Whatever she did worked because Bridget was asleep within half an hour. Carolyn, Joey and I discussed how we would handle Marks drug problem.

We made the call to Mr. Bogan the following Monday night. We got his cell phone number from his office secretary. Joey and I were both afraid of him. He was a big man and this was news he would not want to receive. We were afraid he would take it out on us.

"Hello?" Mr. Bogan answered the phone in an irritated voice.

"Mr. Boga, this is Adam and Joey. We wanted to talk

to you about Mark," I quickly said. His voice seemed to lighten once he realized who had called him.

"Adam, what's wrong?" he spoke softly.

"Mr. Bogan, we know that Mark has been using drugs. First it was weed but there are rumors that he could be using heroine. We didn't believe the rumors till prom night when he started acting really weird," I confused. Joey watched me as we listened for Mr. Bogan to speak next. The moment of silence was released by his long sigh over the phone.

"I had been afraid of this moment for a long time. I knew something was wrong when I smelled the weed at the house. Never would I have imagined he would take it this far though," Mr. Bogan. He sounded tired. "Thank you boys, I genuinely appreciate you telling me this. Now if you'll excuse me, I need to address this problem." Then the phone went silent as the call ended.

Joey and I walked around the neighborhood in silence till it was late at night. We assured ourselves what we did was the right thing for Mark but we both still felt like we betrayed him. Mark was not at school the next day. We wouldn't see him again for quite some time.

CHAPTER EIGHTEEN

Graduating High School

CAROLYN AND I BOTH GOT accepted to University of Iowa. They had arguably the best writing program in the country. We applied to several others as well; Emory, University of Colorado and University of Illinois. We didn't go to visit any of them. The only stipulation to going to a school was that we both get accepted. Carolyn had straight A's in high school. I was very close, but hers were all obtained in advance classes. I never wanted to work that hard.

We both received our acceptance letters in large envelopes on the same day. That was the sign. If you got a small envelope you could expect to read:

Dear Dumb Ass,

The admissions committee has carefully reviewed your application and after much consideration, have come to the conclusion you're not smart enough to be in our presence.

In comparison, our letter read something like:

Dear deity,

You have been granted the opportunity to walk with Angels, your shit doesn't stink and we would gladly bottle your urine for posterity.

What a load of shit. We wanted to be writers. Getting accepted was not success. Getting good grades was not success. Nor was graduation. Success to Carolyn and I was staying together and becoming writers. We didn't need to be Stephen king, or god-forbid, Janet Evanovich. We just wanted to make a living and be together.

The day we received our acceptance letters my family and Carolyn's went out to dinner together; including Mr. Autumn. That made for some interesting table dynamics. Carolyn's parents didn't speak and each of them was noticeably trying to act as happy as pigs in shit. In reality they both looked nervous and miserable. After dinner I had a chance to talk with Mr. Autumn while Carolyn and her mom went to the washroom.

"I'm really proud of you both," he told me

"Thanks, we are excited."

"I wish I had a bigger place," he said "I wish I could be around you guys more." Carolyn would spend a few nights a week at her dads. I never went because I didn't want to impose on the little time Carolyn had with her dad. She loved him like crazy. He worked unbelievable hours as a corporate executive. He paid for Mrs. Autumns life style and probably always would, despite the fact she was known to be a tramp. I felt bad for him.

"We should try and make that happen," I said.

"You take good care of her at school Adam," He said reaching to shake on it.

"I sure will," I told him, meaning it.

Graduation was bittersweet. Joey, Carolyn and I all met at my house before the ceremony. My dad took photos. We hadn't spoken about it but my dad could sense Joey and I were upset.

"You know this is the best for him boys?" he said. Joey quickly agreed. I felt guilty as hell. I still wasn't sure what was good for him since I didn't know where the hell he was. Did his dad send him to rehab, a distant cousins farm, kill him and hide the remains?

"What's best for him? Not graduating high school?" I asked sarcastically.

"You know better Adam," Dad said "Mark is a young man with the world in front of him. Now he has a second chance. Drugs are a dead end road. Something you saw had you worried enough to do something about it. You didn't do it for the fun of it. You three likely saved his life."

The three of us drove to our school where the graduation was to take place. We stuck close as every other person we saw would confront us with questions about Mark. Where he was, if he was going to graduate, if he overdosed, if he was in the hospital? The various rumors had spread like wild fire. Each time we were approached all we could do is lie. I was the one who responded to each inquiry.

"Where's Mark?" asked the first asshole.

"No idea. I know as much as you."

"Is it true Mark overdosed?" asked the second.

"Wouldn't know."

"Heard Mark went nuts bro, is he okay?" asked the third. On and on each person thinking they were really friends with Mark and I so they should be able to get at least a tid-bit of information. Some of them I didn't know at all; hippies Mark had recently befriended. One of them had dreadlocks and smelled like piss. I wanted to get out of there more than anything.

It was hot that morning and we were being funneled into the sweltering gymnasium to line up for the processional to the football field where the ceremony was going to take place. We got separated from each other. We lined up in rows in the gym by last name. I was wearing shorts under the long black robe but was still sweating my ass off. Waiting for the procession to start seemed like an eternity. I spent much of it convincing myself to stay for the ceremony. My 'give a shit level' was dangerously low.

The procession finally started. The class of 1993 dressed in black caps and gowns spilled onto the football field like black coffee. I watched the ceremony as though I was spectator outside myself. A few of the inspirational words from some of the administration would hit a chord, but soon fade back out of tune. The valedictorian in his self-righteous manner bloated on.

"Class of 1993, we have been given all of the tools to go out in the world and succeed. Whether it be in the military, off to college or entering our first real job. Our tool boxes are over flowing."

Someone blew up a beach ball. It took flight and bounced around softly over the student body. It's direction accidental and arbitrary. I watched it closely. A faculty member was finally able to retrieve it when it went out of bounds. Phew, I thought, the embarrassment for the superintendent was over. A few parents clapped when the fun ended.

"Carolyn Autumn" the official read off the long list. Carolyn walked up onto the stage. She received her diploma and shook hands with the superintendent. She found me effortlessly while walking across the stage and a knowing smile appeared on her face.

I was watching Joey cross the stage and almost missed my opportunity to get up when the girl next nudged me in the arm. I quickly realized that most of our row was empty when I sprang to my feet to follow the line. I heard my name announced followed by a cheer from the bleachers where I suspected my family was sitting. I grabbed the fake diploma and didn't even bother smiling for the camera. It just felt good to be done with high school.

That night while getting ready for bed my Dad came in my room. "I know I've said it a few times already today, but I'm proud of you," he said.

"Thanks Dad."

"I have a few things for you," he said handing me two envelopes. The first one I opened contained a little silver rosary ring.

"Keep God close and you'll always be okay," he told me. I looked at the second envelope. It was from Mark. "I don't know what it says. I didn't give it to you earlier because I didn't want to possibly make today any harder for you." My dad ruffled my hair and left, closing my door. I opened the envelope. It was a one page-hand written note.

Adam,

You're probably wondering where I've been. My dad caught wind I was doing drugs. I got carted off to a treatment center in California. I haven't been allowed to communicate with anyone outside of here until today. My counselor told me I had to break all ties from home for a while and focus on getting healthy. I get to write a few letters which they have to review before I can send. I was doing a considerable amount of everything available. I was really sick for a while from coming off the stuff. I'm sorry about prom. I think one of the faculty members there knew I was high and reported me. Not sure when I'll be home. I fucked up... Miss you guys. Please fill Joey in.

I finished the letter and immediately called Joey. I explained that Mark didn't know we had been the ones to snitch.

"What do we do?" he asked

"I don't know. His dad could tell him at any time. If we don't fess up were going to look like real dicks."

"Yeah. I think we should just be honest with him. He sounds like he is happy and he is getting help."

"I think your right, but I don't want to do that while he's in there. We can do that when he gets home... whenever that is." I told him, and Joey agreed.

CHAPTER NINETEEN

Preparing for College

I WAS REALLY STARTING TO LOOK forward to college life
when Carolyn and I did our college shopping together.
Bed sheets, blankets, storage bins, toiletries, coffee maker,
laundry baskets, small TV, basic decorations etc. We both
were staying in the dorms. We weren't in the same dorm,
but the buildings were across from each other. My Mom
and Dad and Carolyn's dad drove us to college. They
rented a small van to pack our stuff into. Carolyn drove
in the van with her Dad.

When we arrived, my parents went with me to set
up my room and Carolyn's Dad helped her. My dorm
room was pretty standard; a bunk bed, two desks and
dressers, a futon and one window with a depressing view.
I unpacked and claimed the lower bunk. It was pretty
nice. I was worried about my roommate though. What if
I didn't like him? The school had provided us with our

roommate's info a few weeks prior in case we wanted to coordinate with them what we each would bring. I didn't reach out to him, and he didn't reach out to me. After settling in, we met back up with Carolyn and her dad and had a final lunch with our parents. There was a campus tour starting at three, and we decided to take advantage of it. We went back to our rooms, took showers and met up at the main library for the tour.

It was hot out and Carolyn showed up wearing a smoking hot white and black sundress. When she looked this good, I was concerned someone would snatch her up from me. There were about fifteen other kids on the tour. It was led by a sophomore girl named Sophie. We began our walk. As Carolyn followed up the end of the group, I grabbed her ass. She turned her head back and smiled at me sexily. I could feel her soft ass through the fabric of the dress. She wasn't wearing underwear. It's a good thing I did because I was getting a boner. We passed McLean Hall, I put my arm around her. We came to Schaeffer Hall, I put my hand on her ass again this time leaving it there. Sophie the tour guide babbled. I kissed her at the biology building and we both knew the tour was over. We held hands and nearly ran back to my dorm. I fumbled with the keys and opened the door. Carolyn went in and I pulled her dress up. Nope, no underwear. She pulled my pants down and I threw her back onto the bed and kissed her deeply, entering her. We were sweating still from the heat outside which made the session even hotter. I relished in the taste of her sweat on her neck and chest. We were lost in each other completely. That's why neither of us was aware that my new dorm mate and his parents had opened the door and entered the room.

"Oh my goodness!" a woman cried out. I jumped up turning to face a small Chinese woman with her husband and son, my roommate behind her. A sure way to end a fuck session, but not a throbbing boner the whole family was staring at.

"You pigs?" she asked.

"No ma'am," I responded.

"Sure. You pigs. Why you doing that here? Who are you?"

"I'm Adam," I told her "and this is my room."

She turned to her son. "You are not staying in this room with the pig. Now get out of here now."

"Wait I'm sorry," I tried to explain but she turned on me.

"Pig, you do not talk to me you hear? I will tell the Dean. Now get away from me!" She stormed out of the room and slammed the door. I looked at Carolyn in amazement.

"Come here you pig!" she shouted.

I jumped back on top of her; we kissed and laughed.

What else could we do? We were busted. I assumed the woman would have marched right down to the Deans office and we would be expelled. She put on a pair of my sweats and we waited for a knock on the door. The knock never came and we didn't get expelled. Getting caught doing it with Carolyn ended up being incredibly fortuitous. The next morning the floor resident assistant Jimmy Taylor, introduced himself in the communal washroom.

"Your Adam right?" he said extending his hand for a shake.

"That's right."

He then briefly informed me of his duties and explained to me his main concerns. "Keep the booze well hidden, never bring it into the hallways. If you're drinking keep your door closed. If you're smoking weed, make a blower and shoot it out the window. Got it?" he asked.

"No problem. I don't really smoke weed," I told him.

"Well, you don't yet. But when you do, blow it out the god-damned window. Okay?"

"I got it. Out the window."

"Now, on to the little issue you got me wrapped up in yesterday. You, my friend have a horse shoe stuck up your ass. You got caught fucking in your room and your roommate's mom throws a fit and can't have her son rooming with a, pig, I think it was. Now what this means is that Chen, your near miss roommate, who has been introduced only to your butt cheeks and erection has been moved to another building. Following me?" he asked

"I'm still with you."

"Good. Because here's where it gets really good. You have now become the luckiest son of a bitch in the history of this dormitory. You get the double room to yourself. The only catch is I get your extra dresser. I need a place to keep some of my shit. You still with me?"

"I am, and I have no problem with the dresser arrangement. I don't have that much stuff."

"Good. Remember, no drinking in the hallways and blow it out the window. I'll be by later today to drop my shit off," he said as he walked out the bathroom.

We spent our last day before classes walking around the campus and conducting our own tour. We found a good little coffee shop and familiarized ourselves with the cafeteria system. Most students were picking stuff up to go and taking it back to their dorm rooms. We had the opportunity to formally meet Chen in the cafeteria that night. We didn't realize he was standing in front of us in the line until he turned around.

"Nice to see you both wearing clothes," he said cheerfully. We both laughed and Carolyn's face reddened.

"Sorry about that," I told him.

"Don't worry about it. My mom can be pretty intense. I'm Chen," he said. We introduced ourselves and paid for our meals. "Would you care to join me?" he asked. We agreed and we found a table and settled in. We all chose the lasagna and dinner roll special. Chen was from San Francisco and was a really nice guy. He said we were lucky since Carolyn and I already knew each other. He said he was nervous to be on his own for the first time and he didn't know a soul.

"You know us," Carolyn said with a smile. "Were friends now aren't we?"

Chen laughed "Yes we are."

We finished dinner and sat around talking for a good while. Chen had a girlfriend back in California. She was a senior this year in high school. She was hoping to come to school here next year if her parents could be convinced. They felt choosing a school because Chen went there was nonsense. We made plans to have dinner with Chen the following evening as well.

Carolyn and I went to her place to pick up her stuff. I had no roommate so we planned to live at my place. I met Carolyn's roommate. She was nothing like Carolyn; polar opposites in fact. Erica was a big girl. She took up a considerable amount of space in the small room. She was friendly enough, but not someone either of us had much in common with. She played the trumpet in the marching band. Carolyn was relieved she wasn't going to have to stay in the little dorm room with her.

Carolyn and I developed our daily rituals our first semester at school. Monday through Thursday it was class in the morning, followed by lunch. Study at the library for a few hours, then my place for a nap. We ate dinner with Chen on most nights and sometimes he joined us in my room for a movie. Watching movies with Chen reminded me of Mark since he and I used to watch movies together often. Chen was also a fan of the movie *Die Hard*, and had demanded we watch it together not once, but twice. On weekends Carolyn and I would go to the coffee house at night with her friend Cindy. Cindy sat next to Carolyn in English Lit 101. They met the first day of class. Cindy spilled a cup of tea on Carolyn when she was trying to get settled into her seat.

The coffee house we frequented was named Jitters. They had open mic nights on Friday and Saturday from nine to ten thirty. We would write prior to kick off. Carolyn and I never got up and read anything. Cindy on the other hand always had something, or several things to read. Her work was depressing and self-loathing. Sometimes her writing would only be a few sentences long. She would pound down some of her tea before walking to the small stage. Grab the mic like she owned it and read.

> *"Two pillows.*
> *A soft mattress*
> *A blanket so warm*
> *This is my cell, my prison, my refuge.*
> *Here in my cell the pain is most bearable.*
> *Convict me of the crime and throw away the key."*

"I don't even like it!" I told Carolyn.

"Shhh. Stop that. She is putting herself out there."

"Yeah, and making me and everyone else in here uncomfortable!" I just didn't get Cindy. She was mentality abused as a child and would carry that angst with her for as long as I would know her. I never could figure out how she was mentally abused. She would say it all the time, but never explain how she was abused.

"Did your dad yell at you all the time?" I asked one time, feeling brave.

"Hah! I wish," she said.

"Ahh. I'm sorry. He was physically abusive?"

"No, no. He never hit me or touched me or anything." She paused "Although, I'm not sure which is worse." Carolyn and I oddly felt as if we didn't fit in sometimes since we weren't mentally abused. "You two don't know what it's like to have had the struggles I've had. I wish I could have grown up all apple pie and shit," she would say, or something similar.

Every time she would drill one of these reminders into us I would whisper to Carolyn. "It's not my fault her father did her wrong." or "Am I supposed to feel guilty my parents didn't get drunk and abuse me?" Carolyn would always hush me and tell me to be understanding. She told me she was her friend and that Cindy needed someone in her life; someone to listen even if they didn't completely understand. Not knowing how hard it would be, I promised I would try. I never expected to find myself in Cindy's position, needing someone desperately to talk to.

CHAPTER TWENTY

A Never Ending Sickness

OUR FIRST SEMESTER WENT QUICKLY and we were looking forward to our first college break. Winter break was two weeks long and we were excited to see our parents. Finals were wrapped up on Wednesday and we would take a bus to Chicago the next day where my Dad would pick us up. After our last final we met Chen for dinner. I didn't feel well and didn't eat. It felt like I still hadn't digested dinner from last night or the water I drank that morning. Like my system just didn't want to process what was sitting there. The cafeteria was buzzing with excitement. Freshman mostly used the cafeteria and everyone was excited to get home for the holiday break. This was a night for celebration. I just wanted to get back to my room and lie down or puke, I wasn't sure which.

"I need to get to my room," I told them.

"Really? That bad huh?" Carolyn asked.

"How about some curdled milk with sardines?" Chen joked.

"Screw you," I said giving him a smile. The plan was for the three of us to meet Cindy at Jitters that night. We had a bottle of whiskey - Irish coffee and poetry. I couldn't make it. My body was giving me increasingly unmistakable cues that it was time to find a washroom. My stomach was turning and the muscles were starting to spasm. Waves of nausea were beginning to wash over me. "I need to get out of here before I either puke all over the two of you or shit my pants. You two go to Jitters without me. I have a date with the toilet and bed tonight."

"I'll go with you," Carolyn offered.

"No, just go with Chen, have fun. No point being around me all night if I am just going to be sick." She kissed me goodbye on cheek and I rushed to the dorm. The timing was spot on. I made it to the toilet as the first wave of vomit hit the water. I was violently ill. After a half hour of retching the RA paid me a visit.

"You okay Adam? A few too many celebratory shots?" he asked.

"I wish. I'm just fucking sick," I told him.

"You need anything?"

"No I'll be okay."

"Alright. Well let me know if you do. I'll be here all night. I'm staying in. You got my number." I thanked him and dry heaved for another 10 minutes before walking to my room.

I got to my room and the chills kicked in. I was freezing. I put on sweat pants, a long sleeve t-shirt and a sweat shirt and got in bed under the covers. This was probably a mistake as I could feel my temperature rising. I had a fever. I don't know how high; I didn't own a thermometer. I took two Tylenol to lower the fever but this turned out to be the wrong choice as I threw up again. I lay in bed, dizzy feeling and out of it. I guessed the fever to be at a hundred and four or so. I was so weak I was shaky every time I stood up. I drifted in and out of a confused sleep.

That was the reason I didn't hear or didn't care to answer the phone that kept ringing. I vaguely remembered it ringing. I heard the knock on my door. I came to enough to creep over and open it. Chen was standing there and something was wrong. He was pacing back and forth in the hallway nonstop. He was breathing hard and tears were rolling down his face.

"Something happened," he told me while still pacing.

"Slow down dude," I said squinting my eyes as my headache rang like a bell. "What are you talking about?"

"Something really bad happened, Adam!" Chen wrapped his arms around me. I felt panic and adrenaline surge through my body. I instantly became angry but very weak and shaky. The mixture of having a high fever and a surge of adrenaline was debilitating. I pushed away and stumbled back to my bed, sitting and putting my head in my hands for support.

"What the fuck are you talking about Chen?!" I asked looking down at my feet. My head felt like it couldn't handle anymore. It was pumping at full capacity.

"Fuck Adam. It's Carolyn. She got hit." *It's a fucking cultural thing. Chen is all worked up. He's overreacting to something. Maybe he's drunk.*

"Are you wasted Chen?" *Chen doesn't drink. Please God. Our Father who art in Heaven...*"What happened Chen? Please just tell me."

"Carolyn got hit by a car outside of Jitters, Adam. I saw it. I don't think she is going to make it. I don't think anyone could."

I got up quickly to find Carolyn and see for myself. I didn't make it to the door before I passed out. I remember coming to several times; the first time to Chen wiping blood off my forehead with a wet cloth with several other people in my room. There was a commotion going on. I tried to sit up remembering what Chen told me about Carolyn. When what he told me internalized, I passed out again. My next memory was of being in an ambulance. It was very bright in the back and there was a paramedic with me. I heard the muffled sound of the siren from above.

"Where is she? Oh my God, where is she?" I asked in a whisper.

"Just relax," she said. I felt a sharp pain in my arm as she inserted the needle to start an IV. This added just enough stress to my already destroyed body to turn the bright box of the ambulance dark again. I drifted off somewhere, and did not wake until the next morning.

When I finally opened my eyes, the first person I made out was my dad, then saw my mom on the other side of my bed. Each of them was holding one of my hands.

"I'm so sorry Adam," my mom said quietly.

"She's dead?" I more stated than asked, still hoping there was a chance I was mistaken, that this was all an awful dream induced by influenza and fever. The room was silent except for my mother's sobs. No answer was needed. My mother slumped onto the bed resting her face in the pillow next to my ear and apologized repeatedly. I cried until it was hard to catch my breath. The doctor came in and reviewed my chart and vitals on the machine next to my bed.

"Adam we're going to give you something through

the IV to help you relax a bit. You're going to need rest. This is a lot to take on without being as sick as you are." My dad thanked him. A few minutes later a nurse came in with a small bottle and added it to my IV cocktail. I soon felt as if I was floating on a cloud. Nothing mattered as I lost all comprehension. I knew my parents were with me and crying but I had forgotten why as I faded back into the darkness. I wanted to just stay there, like in Cindy's bed, or cell or whatever the fuck she called it in the poem.

CHAPTER TWENTY-ONE

Coming Back Into a New Reality

T HE NEWSPAPER REPORT READ:

Carolyn Anne Autumn, a St. Charles resident attending University of Iowa was struck by a vehicle Wednesday on East Washington St., died Wednesday evening according to the Johnson County Coroner. University officials have confirmed the death as a result of head trauma sustained in the accident. Carolyn, 18, was on her way to a meet a friend at a local coffee shop at about 5 p.m. Wednesday. She was standing on the edge of Washington St. near the intersection of Clinton St when a vehicle jumped the curb and struck her. The undisclosed driver has been charged with driving under the influence and manslaughter, Columbia County sheriff's Department confirmed.

The drugs the doctor prescribed to help me relax were strong. I barely remember the trip home with mom and dad. The wake was scheduled for Sunday with the funeral on Monday. I was still very weak from being sick. I lay in bed staring at the geometrical colored lines and shifting shapes, on my computer screen saver for hours on end. The drugs made me a zombie and I felt like I was lost in a fog.

My parents took me to the wake and I sat in the back of the room. They went up to the front to offer their condolences. It was a closed casket. There were more people there than I expected; people who I didn't expect to see. There were high school teachers, kids who she wasn't friends with and family members I never met. Chen and Cindy were there together. Mrs. Autumn and her estranged husband were both at the front of the room receiving hugs and handshakes. I saw my parents talking to Mrs. Autumn. She looked around and caught my eye and instantly started to cry and rushed out of the room. In my drug induced state, I felt disconnected and sunk into a deeper depression. Joey and Bridget had arrived and came to talk to me.

"I'm so sorry." Joey said. Bridget leaned down and hugged me and held on for longer than normal.

"I need to go home." I said staring where Mrs. Autumn and my parents had stood.

"I know buddy. Soon… it will all be over soon." Joey said.

"No. Now. Take me home now," I said standing up and negotiating my way through the crowded room. Several people tried to talk to me. Provide words of comfort I suppose. I waved them off and pushed for the door.

"I'll tell his parents. You take him to your car," I heard Joey tell Bridget.

I got out of the funeral home and started walking aimlessly in the parking lot. Bridget ran to me and held my arm guiding me the other direction to her car parked on the street. She unlocked my door and went around to the driver's side and we got in. I rest my head on the cool window looking for Joey so we could leave.

"I know you don't want to talk about it right now Adam, but if and when you do, I'm here for you," Bridget said.

"Thanks," I said and nothing more. Joey jumped in and they drove me home. I stepped out of the car, thanked them for the ride and went straight to my room. I popped a tranquilizer, stripped to my underwear and laid in bed. The funeral was the next day. I kept telling myself I had to be there. I had to say goodbye properly. I fucked that up today. No matter how weak I still felt I knew I had to suck it up. This was my last chance to say goodbye to Carolyn.

I felt like I could someone reassure Mrs. Autumn that things would be okay, even though I wasn't convinced. The loss was all too new and I didn't know what to say to her. She ran off crying when she saw me. I didn't know why. Was she mad at me for letting this happen to Carolyn? Maybe I should have had her stay with me. I let her go out with that flake Cindy. Maybe I reminded her of the fun times we shared with Carolyn? What would I say to her and what the hell would I say to her dad? I wanted so badly to take the easy way out and not go to the funeral and subject myself to the misery but knew this was wrong. My conscience and the tranquilizer solidified my resolve to attend the funeral, and apologize to Carolyn's parents. I drifted off in my increasingly familiar drug induced haze.

"Got a minute?" my dad asked sitting on the edge of my bed. I sat up leaning my back on my headboard, realizing it was already morning.

"What's going on?" I asked.

"I wanted to talk to you about a few things Adam."

"Sure Dad."

"I know this has been really rough for you. You have been through a lot. You were really sick, and then to have this happen to you is a tremendous shock to your system. I expect you to struggle through this bud, but I also want to talk to you about facing hardship. You've heard the expression a diamond in the rough?"

"Sure"

"Well that's what we should try and be like. When things get tough, we try our best to continue shining. Epictetus said, 'it's not what happens to you, but how you react to it that matters'. I'm not saying you should be upbeat, but I don't want you lost either. I'm worried about you. I've never seen you lost before, and just don't want to. No one should have to go through what you're going through. Time heals buddy, and it will heal this too. Through my life I've had things that hit me hard… when my dad died, when my cousin Rudy died. It just takes time."

"Thanks Dad. It's going to suck for a while." I bit my lip and blinked several times in quick succession fighting back the tears. My dad put his hand on the back of my neck and squeezed.

"Yeah, I know it will. Be careful with those pills too. Just because they help you not feel it now, doesn't mean you're not going to have to deal with it later. Don't get reliant on those things. I know you're smarter than that but it can creep up on you." I knew he was right. It had only been a few days and I was already looking forward to the next pill, so the calm warmth could wash over me. The alternative was the dreadful realization that I would never see Carolyn again. I lost what very well could have been the one for me.

"I'll be careful, thanks Dad."

"We have to leave in an hour. You should jump in the shower. If you can, try and talk to Mrs. Autumn today. It's the right thing to do; give your condolences. I know you're having a hard time facing her. This is one of those things you just need to do. I know she will appreciate it. She thinks the world of you. We spoke yesterday and I'm worried about her too. She told us she feels like she lost everything."

"I don't know what to say to her dad. She did lose everything."

"Tell her you're sorry. Tell her how you feel. She'll understand that. Believe me. Tell her *you* feel like you lost everything. Let her know she's not the only one that feels like that." I thought about what to say the whole time I was getting ready. *I'm sorry and I feel like dying myself* didn't seem like the right thing to tell her. I resented the fact that you have to appear at a wake and funeral. To be put on display for everyone to look at during a time of loss. I realized this shouldn't be about me, it should be about honoring Carolyn, but still felt like a zoo animal being brought out to be witnessed.

My brother John came home from school to be at the funeral. I had rarely seen my brother choked up but when he told me he was sorry that I lost Carolyn, he was barely able to hold back. Having everyone around me so sad highlighted the gravity of the loss making it more difficult. On the way, I had my father stop at the florist. My mom had already sent a large floral arrangement to the wake, but I wanted to buy a few long stem roses. I wanted one to put on Carolyn's casket when they put her in the ground, and I wanted one for Mrs. Autumn. I asked the clerk what I should buy for a funeral and she said white roses were appropriate. She also found it necessary to apologize for my loss and told me white represented purity and mourning. The purity of Carolyn and the mourning of Mrs. Autumn? Mrs. Autumn never seemed quite pure. The sweet smell of the flowers on my lap filled the car and sickened me. The smell of roses would from that day forward remind me only of death.

We arrived and went in the long brick building where the service would be held. I imagined this building had a basement where embalming and the cremation of bodies took place. Several stoic employees in suits were ushering the newcomers to their seats. We were spotted by Mr. Autumn and ushered by him to seats up near the front. Mr. Autumn offered the first words between us.

"I just can't believe this is happening Adam."

"I can't either. I am so sorry. I don't know what to say or what to do." I told him laying it on the table.

"No one does. We shouldn't. This shouldn't happen. It shouldn't have happened to her, to you and it shouldn't have happened to me. It's in God's hands now, that's all I can believe."

"Yeah." Is all I could manage to get out of my mouth as a large lump formed in my throat. I felt like I blew it again and said the wrong thing or didn't say enough. An elderly couple squeezed past me on the way to their seats. They sat next to Mrs. Autumn. Her parents I presumed.

"We are having several readings during the ceremony. Would you be able to read something and assist as a pallbearer?" He asked.

"Of course," I told him. We found our seats and sat down. A surge of fear at the prospect of reading the slip of paper Mr. Autumn gave me washed away my strength. My hands and feet became cold and clammy. I made a quick trip to the washroom for some water to rinse down a pill and a half. In ten minutes the prospect of reading my assignment would be less traumatizing.

The pastor leading the ceremony was a slight old

man with pale-ashen features. His greasy greying hair matched his face. He read several passages and talked about being gentle with each other during delicate times. I rehearsed in my head what I was asked to read over several times so I wouldn't trip over my words. Then he called me by name to read. I walked reluctantly towards the podium, my movements feeling stiff and awkward. I looked to Mrs. Autumn who gave me a slight smile easing my concern by a fraction and giving me hope. I read from the paper:

> *Do not stand at my grave and weep*
> *I am not there, I do not sleep*
> *I am a 1,000 winds that blow*
> *I am the diamond glints on snow*
> *I am the sun on ripened grain*
> *I am the gentle autumn rain*

My concentration broke for a moment. I made eye contact again with Mrs. Autumn needing to see she was okay. She gave me the smallest, almost undetectable, reassurance in the form of a slow blink. I knew what it meant. It was like I was communicating with Carolyn, reading each other's minds like lovers can often do. It meant *I'm okay, finish it*. I read the same line again before continuing on.

I am the gentle autumn rain
When you awaken in the morning's hush
I am the swift uplifting rush
Of quiet birds in circled light
I am the soft star that shines at night
Do not stand at my grave and cry
I am not there...

The last line of the poem read *I did not die*. I ended the poem leaving off the last words. The words were not true and I knew Carolyn would have agreed that I not read them. Cindy later agreed with me when I shared with her what I had done. Those words I could hear Carolyn say were bullshit. She was dead, and there was no sense even metaphorically pretending otherwise.

I took my seat feeling slightly confidant that I had in some small way pleased Mrs. Autumn. I had these recurring feelings that I had done something wrong and she was mad at me. That in some way I was the cause of Carolyn's death. After all, I was at school with Carolyn. Both our parents had told us to take care of each other. Hell, I would have taken care of her, and this likely would not have happened if I hadn't gotten the flu. I would have been with her and wouldn't have let her be so close to the street, or could have seen the car coming and pulled her away. When the pills would start to wear off the self blame would intensify. I tried to keep telling myself that I was sick and couldn't get out of bed. You can't be with someone twenty four hours a day, this could have happened while she was on her way to class. I couldn't possibly be with her all the time. I know this all made sense and I needed to come to terms with the fact I had done nothing wrong. This was rehashed in my head over and over again all day.

I put on the white gloves I was given and approached the casket. It was sparkling grey with silver handles. I questioned whether she would have liked it. *Who the fuck cares?* She probably can't see it anyway. Why don't people pick out their caskets before they die? Wouldn't you want to choose where and how your body will rest in perpetuity? I should write a will with detailed instructions. No, who gives a shit. *Why am I putting on these gloves?*

We lifted the coffin off the cart and carried it to the hearse. It was surpassingly light. We slid it into the back and the driver closed up the door. It was a short drive across the road to the plot where Carolyn would be buried. I got in the car with my family and we drove over. My anxiety and sadness building during the short trip. This was the last of it. After this there was no more Carolyn. No more honoring her memory or being close to her fallen body. I hated being at the wake and the way

I felt at the funeral. Once it was all over, I knew I would be alone and I was afraid of the finality of it all.

Cars parked where they could along the side of the narrow road in the cemetery. Mourners spilled out of their cars in their best black attire. We approached the gravesite where the casket was already on its mechanical perch above the hole dug in the dirt. A green skirt hid the dirty mess beneath where she would spend the decades to come. I looked around the landscape considering if Carolyn would have liked the location. A row of chairs were set up in front of the grave; Mrs. and Mr. Autumn were among the occupants. The service at the grave was very brief, an introduction to the final resting place.

Everything worth saying had already been said. After a final prayer I began to cry. It was the saddest I had been up to this point. Previous emotions were a mixture of grief, shock, anger, disbelief and confusion. I was left with only grief. I still had two flowers to deliver. I took them from John who was doing his best to hold back the tears that began to run down his face. I walked to the grave and placed a flower on top of the casket. I laid my hand on top and rubbed the smooth lacquered surface. I said the Our Father and prayed the Lord take care of Carolyn.

"I love you so much." I said one last time.

I looked up to find Mrs. Autumn on the other side of

the casket wiping the tears from her eyes with a tissue. I walked around to her.

"I'm so sorry," I said

"I know. I know... we all are," she said, losing composure as she spoke.

"I just don't know what to say, or what to do," I said. Mrs. Autumn put her arms around me. I held her back. It was the first time since I heard what had happened that I felt a non-drug induced relief. It was as if I held Carolyn, or part of her. I didn't want to let go.

"I miss her so much it hurts," I said as tears filled my eyes. She squeezed tighter.

"I'm here for you Adam. We can be here for each other." We released each other and sat in the chairs in front of the casket as people walked to their cars to leave. My family and the Autumns stayed. We sat, watched and cried as they lowered Carolyn down into the cold dark earth.

CHAPTER TWENTY-TWO

Coming Out of the Fog

AFTER THE FUNERAL, THE REST of my two week winter break consisted of lying in bed. I felt exhausted and couldn't maintain any sustained level of energy. I had no sense of time. I kept my room dark. I often woke up unsure whether is was day or night. I felt drawn to see Mrs. Autumn. She said she was there for me, but I couldn't get the courage to face her again. I was still struggling with the recurring feelings it was my fault somehow.

We celebrated Christmas to some extent although I barely remembered it. My father had brought the TV from the den into my room so I could watch instead of staring at the computer screensaver, but I didn't watch. We hadn't talked about returning to school until the Friday before classes were to resume. My dad came to see me in my room, which had begun to take on a funny smell; the smell of living in a small area day after day.

"I don't want to go back Dad."

"I know it's hard right now Adam, but believe me, going back will help you work through all of this."

"I don't think so Dad. Everything about Iowa reminds me of Carolyn. We did everything together there. I am really scared to go back."

"What about your friends there? Try and get back into the swing of things."

"My friends there all revolved around Carolyn, Dad. I never hung out with them without her."

"Adam, we move on. That's what we do. We have to. I've told you this before, and I'll say it again. Do hard things."

"I know Dad, and I usually try to. But I just can't snap out of it this quick."

"I've already called and spoken to one of the campus grief counselors. Their aware of what you are going through and they are going to be there for you. They know how to help people cope with this kind of loss. That's what they do." We sat quite for several minutes. I had nothing else to offer. I had no fight left in me. I wanted to be alone. I decided it might be easier making that happen in Iowa than it would be at home.

"Okay. I'll go back. I don't fucking want to, but fine. I'll go back. Now can I go back to sleep?"

My dad squeezed my hand. "You're making the right choice bud." I went to bed and slept.

I woke up at ten and went downstairs to get something to eat when I heard my parents arguing in my mom's office over whether going back to Iowa was the right choice. My mom thought a fresh start away from Iowa and the memories I had there might be best. My dad told her it was something I had to face and I couldn't just quit when things got tough. I was pissed at my father for suggesting I had to "face" what I now considered the revolting State of Iowa. As if going to Iowa, and reliving all the memories of the times Carolyn and I shared would somehow make it all hurt less. My mother didn't escape my petulance either. Her opinions indicated to me she thought I wasn't capable of overcoming this and had I had to be shielded or protected like a child. Reconciling these inexplicable emotions was far beyond what I was capable of so I went back to bed hungry. I lost weight over the past few weeks. I ate only when I needed too. I ate when it hurt.

I had come home from the university so fast I hadn't packed anything. Everything I needed for school was still in my dorm. On Sunday my father drove me back to Iowa. We had a late lunch and said our tearful goodbyes. It was harder to say goodbye this time. I wanted to be alone but was afraid of it at the same time. When my family came to visit me at home I wanted to be alone. But now, I questioned how I would feel if no one came to visit. Would I spiral into a deeper depression if that was possible?

I went to my dorm room and climbed into bed. The next day classes resumed. I stayed in bed staring at *Andy Griffith* reruns. Not by choice, that's just what seemed to be on most of the day. I had followed my father's advice and stopped taking the pills. I kept them close by as insurance. It was comforting to know I had them. If I chose, relief was only ten minutes away.

A week passed. More *Any Griffith* reruns. I would get up to get food from the cafeteria or to go to the washroom; otherwise I stayed in bed. I avoided Chen and Cindy who had stopped by several times. When I heard their knocks on the door I would creep over and look out at them through the peephole. The phone was beginning to ring more often. I could hear my dad and the squeaky voiced grief counselor leave me messages. I called my dad back a few times to let him know I was okay. I didn't call the grief counselor back. This turned out to be a poor choice as it earned me a visit, or in counselor's parlance, a "wellness check".

When the counselor arrived at my door, I knew who she was without asking. She wore a brown pantsuit and had a wooden cross around her neck. I imagine she was a volunteer from a local church or something. When I peeked out at her through the peek hole, I saw she wasn't alone. She was with the Jimmy Taylor, the resident assistant. This meant two things, first Jimmy had a key and they would be opening the door if I didn't, and second I was going to have to talk to this lady, which I was in no mood to do. Realizing there was no point in delaying the inevitable, I opened the door.

"Adam?" the woman asked.

"That's me"

She stepped forward and extended her hand. Jimmy stepped back as if I was contagious. I sensed he was uncomfortable and didn't know what to say. "I'm Mary Norton," she said with a smile extending her hand. I took it and gave it a limp noodle of a shake. She compensated for it by squeezing much harder than I imagined her slight frame capable of. "You and I are going to get along famously," she said. "Jimmy thanks for showing me the way. I'll ring you if I need you." Mary had an Irish accent and instantly intrigued me. She was very plain and slight in appearance but had an undeniable presence. She struck me as someone who knew exactly what she was doing. This prospect comforted me because I felt so lost.

She walked into my room and looked around. "It stinks in here. Let's go for a walk," she suggested. I had pointed out early in our walk that people seemed to be looking at us so we walked the perimeter of the campus. News of Carolyn's death had spread around campus, and those who lived in my building knew who I was and wanted a glimpse of me. Its human nature I guess.

"You haven't been going to class," she commented.

"I haven't felt much like doing anything. I didn't want to come back."

"Why did you?"

"My dad I guess. He said I had to get on with life."

"Maybe you should have stayed home."

"And piss my dad off? Listen to him bitch all the time?"

"You can't make everyone happy all the time Adam. Sometimes you have to do what feels right for you. Was coming back to school and lying in your bed all week going to make your father happy?"

"Uh no. He doesn't know."

"He will soon enough. You can't miss many more days before they will drop you from the classes."

"I just have no interest in anything right now. I feel

like I need more time. Everything here reminds me of her," I said holding back tears.

"Then take it. The school has a program where you can take up to a year off for a significant life event. It allows you to basically take the break you need to get things back on track."

"Really?" I said. I felt an enormous sense of relief that the grief counselor actually supported the way I felt. She stopped walking and faced me. She looked different now. She looked more like a friend than an enemy.

"If you feel like you need time away from here, then take it Adam. If you don't ever want to come back after your break, don't. It's your life. Everyone grieves in a different way. It may not seem like it now, but you're going to get over this. You may always remember, and remembering may bring back some sorrow, but mostly the holes left from this will be filled over. You know what they say about death and taxes?"

"No, I don't." I admitted

"Well no matter, just trust me when I say in the grand scheme of things this is a fairly large bump in the road, but one you're on your way over. There's no right way to do this. The Kübler-Ross model details the five stages of grief that many people experience. Some experience a few of the five stages, some experience all of them. The five stages are denial, anger, bargaining, depression and finally acceptance."

"We studied this is high school," I said. "I think I've been through four of those five about twenty times over the past few weeks."

"That's good. That means you're making progress. Acceptance, naturally is the one you're going to find in due time." We started walking again and wandered the perimeter of the campus until we were back at my building. She walked me back inside and gave me her card and told me to call her if I ever wanted to talk.

"I can call your parents for you and talk to them about you coming back home for a while. I think I can make that easier for you," she suggested.

"I would appreciate that."

"Done. I will call them this evening. Why don't you follow back up with them in the morning?" I thanked her for helping me out and she hugged me goodbye. "You're going to be okay," she promised me before I closed the door. I sat down on my bed and cried out of relief that I would be leaving Iowa and the memories we created there. It felt as though going back home was what I needed to feel better. Like being home would be the magic pill.

My father made the drive back to Iowa the next day to pick me up with a small rental truck. I'd packed all my belongings and those of Carolyn's that she kept at my room. Toiletries mostly. I wanted to see how Mrs. Autumn was doing. I thought giving her some of her things from college would be a good excuse to stop by. I was nervous to see her again.

The drive home went better than I had expected. I thought my dad would have been disappointed in me for coming back home. Mary must have said the right things.

"I'm happy you're coming home," my dad finally said after a long silence.

"Thanks for understanding," I said. "I hope I didn't let you down."

"I'm so proud of you Adam, you haven't let me down. Your going to get through this. Your mother and I are going to be there for you. We always will."

I took a deep breath, thankful to have a father like my dad and looked out the window. The view on the ride home consisted of almost entirely farmland. No signs of life, just field after field of dead crops.

CHAPTER TWENTY-THREE

Homecoming

My parents were pretty understanding for the first week. Bringing my meals to my room and not bothering me with the phone calls that were coming in from friends and extended family. The next Monday, my dad gave me the inevitable talk I had been waiting for. The one where he again explains, I need to move on and snap out of "my funk". I knew he was right; I just wasn't able to do it. I had never been depressed before, this was a very new sensation for me. I had never thought of suicide before. Now I was thinking about it all the time. The problem was I wasn't thinking about doing it, I was obsessing about not doing it. I began to spend most of the day worrying I would get to the point that I actually did consider suicide. I knew this was nonsense but couldn't stop the cycle. I told my dad about it.

"You're sensitive Adam. Just like I am. We're similar

you and I. It can be a curse but it also makes us who we are. Sometimes you got to just get angry when you get feeling down and decide to get on with things. Piss on it! Sometimes you just say piss all over all of it!" This wasn't the first time my father told me this. The first time I got a detention at school I cried my eyes out. I was inconsolable. Dad finally got enough of the crying and hollered at me to piss all over them!

"I'm going to try Dad. I'll get out of the house today," I promised.

I still remember what Mrs. Autumn told me at the funeral. *I'm here for you Adam.* I missed Carolyn so much. Mrs. Autumn was the closest I would ever come to Carolyn again. I hoped to capture a taste of Carolyn in Mrs. Autumn. I *had* even mistaken Mrs. Autumn for Carolyn before in the backyard by the pool I told myself.

I got out of bed and showered. I put on some decent clothes and made myself presentable. I met my Dad in the kitchen as I tried to grab something quick to eat.

"I'm going to go visit Mrs. Autumn today and drop off some of Carolyn's things," I announced after I had finished eating.

"That sounds like a good idea. I bet it would do you some good," he said surprised. "You know you should also give Joey and Mark a call. I bet they would be thrilled to hear from you." My Dad didn't know that Mark was still out of state at rehab. Joey had stayed home to attend community college to be with Bridget who was a year younger and finishing her last year of home school.

I walked slowly towards the Autumn house. I was nervous to see her again. I wanted to be reminded of Carolyn, but was afraid of being reminded *too* much of her. The house seemed sad and deserted even though it was well cared for. I began to feel very depressed. I considered if houses could have emotions and if this one was in despair. I reached my hand into my pocket and fingered the last few pills I had from my prescription and considered taking one to shake the dismal feeling that was beginning to take hold. I decided to push through it and rang the doorbell out of desperation to move on to the next thought or sequence of events. *Just keep moving. Go through the motions and this anxiety will pass.* I had to ring the doorbell twice before I saw signs of life through the decorative door window.

Mrs. Autumn came to the door and opened it. She looked like she hadn't gotten out of bed or off the couch. She was wearing sweat pants and a tank top. She wasn't wearing makeup, which was very uncharacteristic of her. She gave me a smile, the kind that says a thousand words. I smiled back and it must have been a similar type of smile because she hugged me and began to cry. *Here we go again* I thought, and I started to cry with her. She slammed the door shut with one hand and then led me by my hand to the large sectional couch where she offered me the corner seat. I sat down and she sat next to me with her knees pulled up to her chest. I kept wiping at my eyes trying to clear the tears.

"Want to watch something funny?" she asked. "Maybe it will help."

"Sure."

"I don't know how to kill the time Adam."

"I know. I don't either. I haven't been able to get out of bed hardly."

"Wait a second, why aren't you at school?" she asked.

"I can't go back there Mrs. Autumn. Everything reminds me of her."

"Imagine staying here," she said getting up and going to the TV. She put a movie in. "It's *Trading Places* with Eddie Murphy. Carolyn liked this movie," she said.

The movie began and I leaned back and put my feet up on the ottoman and made myself more comfortable. I felt at ease for the first time in several weeks. I watched the movie and even smiled at times. I felt the hurt still, but somehow I felt like half the burden was lifted; as if Mrs. Autumn had taken on part of the pain. I wondered if she felt the same way. I finally built up the courage and tried to explain it to her.

"I feel better when I'm here with you. Like I'm with

a part of *her.*" She didn't say anything, but I know she felt the same way because she lied down and put her head in my lap. She took my arm and wrapped it around her and held my hand. I choked up again and took a deep breath holding my emotions at bay. I felt almost normal again holding her hand. I closed my eyes let myself believe I was holding Carolyn.

We had both fallen asleep. When we woke up it was getting dark out. It was the longest uninterrupted sleep I had had in a long time. Mrs. Autumn was lying next to me on the couch and I had my arm around her still. I was afraid to move in fear of waking her. Her back was against me and I could smell her hair and feel the contour of her body against mine. *She feels so much like Carolyn.* A more delicate and sophisticated model of her. I closed my eyes and again tried to prolong the feeling and take it in.

I was a firm believer now in taking in any happiness I could get. Without thinking I expressed this happiness by squeezing her and bringing her in tight to me. She responded by wiggling in even closer to me and putting her hand on my arm that held her. I dared not move in fear of disturbing her or ruining the moment. I fell asleep again and didn't wake until ten. When I got up, she was gone. I went into the kitchen and walked toward the entryway and could hear the sound of the shower running upstairs. I stood there a few moments. I could hear the lonely sound of a grandfather clocks relentless ticking, and felt the emptiness of the house, I once had so many great memories of.

I didn't want to impose on her and still be there when she got out of the shower. I wrote her a note and left it on the counter. *I didn't want to be a bother anymore. Went home. Thanks for everything.*

I lay in bed thinking about where this all could lead to. Why did I feel okay while I was with Mrs. Autumn? Was it because she was like Carolyn, was it because she was a woman and I considered her sexy? The latter made me feel guilty, and even more so because she was her mother. What was the end game here? I couldn't date Mrs. Autumn. She was too old and doing so would be so utterly inappropriate my parents would disown me. All I knew was that I wanted to see her again first thing in the morning.

I worried about Mrs. Autumn's age and the maturity that comes with age. I wanted to drop in unannounced and see her. Adults don't work that way. There are social graces, propriety and my parents to worry about. I worried my parents would be asking about the long hours I spent with Mrs. Autumn. I considered what I would tell them. *See Dad I went over there and we watched a movie. We both fell asleep and then I spooned her, keeping my erection at bay of course.* That wouldn't go over well. As I slept my dreams were filled with Mrs. Autumn. Her or a combination of her and Carolyn. In my dreams I couldn't differentiate between the two. I was holding them in my arms. In my dreams the lines blurred and they became one. In my dreams, I found peace because she wasn't gone. Not completely.

I woke up to the disappointment of reality. My reality was if I wanted to feel close to Carolyn today, and lessen the pain, I would have to find my way back to Mrs. Autumn. Based on yesterday's event, I thought there was a chance that she felt the same way. I had an awful feeling that what happened yesterday was just a fluke, a moment of weakness, a lapse in judgment on her part. I worried that today she would realize that spending time with me, intimate time, was wrong. She had to find it wrong. I was her daughter's first love and she had shared intimacy with me. I'm a young man and she's, well a mature woman with all the responsibilities and hang-ups that come along with it.

Breakfast was offered by my father, but I refused. I lay in bed thinking, or more obsessing like a prepubescent teen about seeing Mrs. Autumn, only sex wasn't the primary concern. It was just her companionship. I wanted to head over first thing in the morning and see her like I would do with Carolyn. I waited, as to not be *too* eager or to become a nuisance to her. At noon my father called me for lunch. I knew I had to oblige. Failing to do so would earn me a good heart to heart and I didn't need that. Not now.

"How you doing champ?" my dad asked. I thought about the Mr. Champ lure embedded in Mark's lip. I felt much like Mark had wearing the lure. Like crap, yet strangely I had the butterflies. The type you have for a new love interest. Like the ones I had for Carolyn when we first hooked up. Except she was gone and her mom remained.

"I'm fine Dad."

"You got a lot of rest lately. I suppose that's a good thing. I think sometimes your body tells you what you need."

"Yeah. I think so too," I didn't want to talk about Carolyn, how I felt, or explain my sleep patterns. In this regard I wished I was back at school.

"Mrs. Autumn called while you were sleeping," I dropped my spoon in my cereal.

"Why didn't you wake me?" I asked irritated.

My dad looked at me concerned. "I thought you needed your rest. You were over there late. I figured you left something or she still needed some yard work"

I sighed. "Alright. Dad if she calls, just please tell me. Please just call for me okay?"

My Dad paused. "Okay Adam, I'll call you."

With that he left the kitchen. I could sense that he felt defeated. I didn't want to deal with it. Before this all happened I would have talked it out with my dad; one of my best friends. But now, I was hiding something. I was in a dark place to begin with and knew it was getting worse. I knew what I wanted, and wanting to be with Mrs. Autumn was ultimately just not possible. I showered and got dressed in comfortable clothes and went straight to her anyway. I didn't call, I just went. It was two in the afternoon when I started towards her house.

On my short walk there I noticed that I looked like I just woke up and rolled out of bed in my sweat pants and t-shirt. When I rang the bell, Mrs. Autumn opened the door and looked the same. She was wearing pink sweatpants and a tank top. Her hair was a mess, but in a sexy, almost deliberate way. I felt angry observing this. Why her? Why is her mom so much like her? She smiled at me and shook her head, turned and walked into the TV room. I shut the door and followed her. She laid down and we resumed the position that would become our daily ritual for the days and weeks to come. Her lying on her side head propped on a pillow and I beside her spooning her while we watched movies.

On one occasion we watched a network marathon of the *I Love Lucy*. Neither one of us even liked the show. Mostly we thought about Carolyn. At times for me at least, I thought about where I was touching Mrs. Autumn. Wrapping my arms around her proved to be acceptable.

In an effort at times to keep the blood circulating I would change positions during a nap and would find my hands around her stomach. Was my hand holding her stomach, or was it touching her breast? Afraid to move I would just hold still and wonder. Over the time spent wasting away on the couch I became bolder.

The first time I took the plunge and wondered if I had crossed the border of acceptability was when she was asleep and I cupped her right breast. She shifted a little finding comfort and settled in. I began to latch on to her breast from then on automatically. I felt like an infant suckling a mother but with my hand; finding comfort in touching her there. I left at around ten each night but one Friday night *she* changed the routine. I stood up to leave and she reached out and took my hand and walked me upstairs to her room. She led me to her bed where I sat on the edge. She went into her closet and a few moments later came out wearing a short silk nightgown. I sat up and she climbed into bed and she straddled me. I rubbed my hands up her body onto her breasts. The feeling of her soft body and silk was intoxicating. She kissed me softly and we let go of all inhibition. It was the most gentle and meaningful love I had ever made. With Carolyn it was fun and loving, but this was different. We were using each other; both getting what we needed. I was with Carolyn again, and to her, I was the closest thing to Carolyn she knew.

CHAPTER TWENTY-FOUR

My Wake-Up Call

THE NEXT MORNING I WOKE with the scent of Carolyn on my skin. For a moment it was just like we were back in college, every morning waking to the smell of each other. But as my eyes focused, I saw Mrs. Autumn lying next to me instead of the love of my life. *What had I done* I thought as I rolled away from her and quickly gathered my clothes. I was careful to dress without waking her and slipped out of the room and out the front door.

The sun was barely over the horizon as I walked silently home. It was early enough that no one would notice the miserable condition I was in as a tears streamed down my face. I had given into temptation in the pursuit of reconnecting with Carolyn. Instead of the comfort I longed for, I was left feeling guilty for dishonoring her memory. I wondered if she had watched me make love to her mother from the gates of Heaven. *Did I share tears with her this morning?*

Reaching my house I was surprised to find Mark sitting on the front steps. For a moment I was nervous he had been there all night and my antics had caused me to miss his homecoming.

I tried to clean up my face on the back of my sleeve, hoping I didn't appear as weak as I felt. I smirked when I noticed he was eating a big bag of potato chips.

"Want some?" he offered as I plopped down beside him. I shrugged my shoulders as I grabbed a handful and started eating in the silence that formed between us.

"How long have you been in town?" I finally asked.

"Just got in yesterday. When I couldn't sleep, I walked over this morning," Mark explained as he set the bag aside. I assumed he would be saving them for later, but I appreciated him sharing some with me.

"You doing okay?" I asked concerned.

"I am actually. I'm doing really well right now," He said.

I felt a wave of relief come over me. I was concerned he had blown off rehab or something.

"Hot date last night?" he jested.

"Something like that," I muttered.

"Spill the beans," Mark said with a smirk.

"I've been spending time with Mrs. Autumn a lot

lately. Being around her is like being around Carolyn…
like she isn't dead and just hanging out down the street,"
I started as I looked down at my hands. I felt filthy and
wanted nothing more than to shower and scrub my skin
raw. "But the more time I spent with Mrs. Autumn, the
more I forgot who she was and spent more time imaging
she was Carolyn…so when she led me to her bedroom
last night it just felt familiar like the many times I had
gone to bed with Carolyn."

Instead of some sly remark about how I had scored
with an older woman, Mark pulled me to my feet and led
us down the sidewalk. I suppose he wanted to get away
from the house in case one of my parents overheard my
pitiful addiction to Carolyn's memory.

"I get it, Adam. I got fucked up on drugs trying to
erase the reality of my parents divorcing. You were doing
the same thing in your own way. You were returning to
Autumn the only way you knew." He put his arm around
my shoulder, and as I thought about his words I noticed
my Mr. Champ lure dangling from his wrist.

"Are you kidding man? You still have that thing?"
I exclaimed as I caught his wrist and looked over the
makeshift bracelet. He tugged it away.

"It was my way of keeping you guys close when I went
to rehab. I missed you guys and this lure kept me looking

forward to getting things back to normal." I looked ahead of us and noticed Joey coming down the street.

He ran up to greet us and we continued walking down the street like nothing had changed since the day we jumped off the back of the school bus.

"Mark there something I need to tell you." I said as I looked over at Joey. He nodded his head knowing what I had to say. Mark looked at me and waited for me to speak. "It was Joey and I that narc'd on you...we were the ones that called your father and told him about the drugs." I wanted the sidewalk to open up and swallow me whole as I waited for Mark to say something.

Mark thought for a few moments. "Thank you? I mean, yes, Thank you." Mark said as he gave Joey a soft punch in the arm. I exhaled deeply finally feeling like a huge burden was finally lifted.

"So let me tell you about this chick I hooked up with at rehab" Mark started.

I returned home later that morning, avoiding my family as I run upstairs to shower and change clothes. Even though it wasn't obvious what I had done last night, I still felt the guilt on my skin where the scent of Mrs. Autumn still lingered. After I had convinced myself I was finally clean, I went downstairs and plopped down at the table. My father was standing over the sink, looking out the window as Scooter entered our yard without his owner. I heard my father say a strange curse word as he turned and finally saw me.

"Hey, son. You hungry? I have apple strudels just out of the oven." he said as he took a seat next to me. I smiled as the familiar scent of baked apples and cinnamon.

"Yeah Dad, I would like that."

"You want some vanilla ice cream to go with it?" he asked.

"Sounds great," I said. "I was with Mark and Joey this morning," I continued as I began thinking of how I was going to explain my plan to my dad. I had made a decision during my morning walk as Mark had made up some bullshit story about this chick from rehab.

"That's great to hear. How are those two doing?"

"Joey is doing good at school and it sounds like him and Bethany are really hitting things off."

"That's nice," my Dad simply remarked as he got up to prepare the plates of strudel. "And how is Mark?"

"He seems to be doing a lot better. He said he is returning to California next week. He found construction work out there and wants to stay close to the rehab center for support. He asked if I wanted to go with him," I announced as he set a plate in front of me, the apple strudel still steaming as the vanilla ice cream quickly melted around it. "And what do you think? Are you going to find work in California too?" my father countered. He was always the logical one.

"I want to go back to school and study writing like Carolyn and I always talked about. I might not have her any more, but I still have our dream," I said as I set the rest of my pills on the table. "I'm ready to start making new memories that Carolyn would be proud...I want to become the person she would be proud of." My father picked up the bottle and went over to the kitchen sink where he washed the pills down the disposal. It made a horribly loud noise as he flipped the switch, the sound of metal grinding rocks. We heard my brother shouting from the basement steps we were making too much noise. We both chuckled as my Dad sat down to enjoy the strudel with me.

I made Mark stop at the cemetery before we started our drive out West. I hadn't returned to Mrs. Autumn's house in fear of falling week again. Mark had explained that the only way to kick an addiction was to remove yourself from the triggers that make you want to use. In my case, I needed to get away from the places that made me think of Carolyn. Before I left town, I had to say good-bye to her one last time.

This time I brought with me a bouquet of wild flowers and the journal we had written in on our way to Millinocket. The trees in the cemetery were shedding their autumn leaves. I smelled the bouquet and was relieved it was not the smell of roses that I wanted to forget from the funeral home. I stooped down and placed the flowers on the top of Carolyn's headstone and the journal over her grave. I said a silent 'good-bye' as I kissed my fingers and placed them on the headstone. Then I turned away and walked back to the car and our journey to California.

I was sitting on the beach watching the waves come in as I chatted with Joey on the phone. The wind was chilly as I sat on the cool sand with a blanket wrapped tightly around my body. My toes were tucked underneath the sand to provide some warmth. Over the last few weeks I had become accustomed to the cooler weather and wind coming off the Ocean. Mark and I had found a small apartment a couple blocks away with other students. We didn't have to share a room so the arrangement was working out good so far.

"Yeah man" Joey said. "I saw Mrs. Autumn with this young guy at the restaurant Bethany and I were eating out at last night. Kind of creepy. This guy was probably half her age. He's obviously into cougars," Joey explained, giving me the latest news from home and Mrs. Autumn's latest antics in town. It seemed to me she had moved on, and though she was still acting like a tramp, at least now she was getting out of the house and off the couch. Perhaps that night together had helped us both move on and accept the fact that Carolyn was gone.

"Well Joey, at least some things don't change" I said as I watched a familiar girl walking up the beach. I had seen her almost every time I would come out to sit on the beach in the evenings. We exchanged waves like normal, but I was surprised when she started walking towards me. "I better go. School starts tomorrow and I still need to get my books." I ended the call as I continued to watch her. She had long brown hair swept down one side of her face. She held it in place with her hand as the breeze blew. From her other hand swung a pair of sandals. I could smell a slight hint of a sweet scent coming off her hair or lotioned body. I felt my heart start to race as I realized how much she looked like Carolyn.

"I've seen you sitting in this same spot almost every night," she said as she plopped down on the sand next to me, pulling her knees up to her chest and holding her toes.

"I love the view," I said

"That makes two of us," she admitted turning her head to look out over the ocean.

"I just moved here to attend University of California," I said. "I'm taking a few online courses till the spring semester."

"It's funny how the locals don't come out to the beach on colder days. Since I moved here I come to the beach every chance I get" she remarked as she slid her hands into her thick sweater.

"What do locals normally do?" I asked as I looked at her face and then into her eyes. Studying them I realized she didn't look like Carolyn. She was beautiful, and that was the similarity.

"I think you'll find that nothing is normal around here. Bunch of messed up people in a messed up world," she said as she pulled her hair back into a pony tail, exposing her neck. I resisted the urge to lean over and plant a kiss on her skin just to see if it was as soft as Carolyn's.

"Sounds pretty normal to me," I remarked as I turned away from her. I had traveled all this way to forget Carolyn and here I was fantasizing about her again. Suddenly I felt wetness in my ear and quickly recoiled as she pulled her finger away from me. "What the hell was that for?" I asked.

"You look like you needed to smile," she said as she

stood and started off down the beach. I watched her stroll gracefully away before I finally let myself smirk. After a few more moments, I gathered my blanket and ran down the beach after her.

ABOUT THE AUTHOR

B ORN AND RAISED IN THE Chicago suburbs, John
Richards resides with his wife, two children and two
German Shepherds. A litigation attorney by trade, John's
favorite way to spend his spare time is with his family and
friends. John is an avid reader and adept daydreamer. He
loves to write and spend his weekends camping. John is a
firm believer that truth is stranger than fiction.

For information on other books visit
www.johnrichardsauthor.com

www.ingramcontent.com/pod-product-compliance
Lightning Source LLC
Chambersburg PA
CBHW020613180626
46810CB00007B/2757